# HONEY GOLD

# LINDSAY MARIE MILLER

Praise for *EMERALD GREEN*

"I loved this book! ...one of the best romance novels I have read in a while"

—*Nerd Girl*

"...this one definitely hit the spot. I can't wait for the next book...!"

—*Kylie's Fiction Addiction*

"This book was all kinds of amazing. I loved every word of it. Sooo good!"

—*Amazon Reviewer*

"I can't wait to get my hands on the next book. I need more!!"

—*Amazon Reviewer*

"This book is awesome! I can't wait to read what happens in the next story."

—*Amazon Reviewer*

"This author is incredibly talented... This was an amazing five star read! This book was SO good! I can't wait to see what happens next in the series!!"

—*Amazon Reviewer*

DON'T MISS THESE OTHER BOOKS BY
LINDSAY MARIE MILLER

*The Girl in the Woods*

*Emerald Green*

*Me & Mr. Jones*

*Mr. Jones & Me*

*Jungle Eyes*

*Island Smile*

*Coastal Spirit*

*Single*

*An Arrangement*

*An Accident*

*Mercy*

AND LOOK FOR HER NEW NOVEL

Available in January 2018

For my loving father:

You held up a mirror, so I could

see the world as it is.

Thank you for listening.

~ ~

# Preface

Voices. All around me. Everywhere.

I take another step into the forest, plunging deeper into darkness. Wind rustles through the trees, sending leaves across my bare feet. My hands circle the goosebumps springing up all over my arms in an effort to ease the sting of loneliness.

A tree snaps behind me as I spin around, missing a large branch. When it lands on the ground with a noticeable thud, I flinch. Wild dogs howl in the distance and I gaze up at the starless sky. The clouds part as I wince from the light of the full moon.

"You killed her! Didn't you? You killed her! You killed her!"

Blood runs deep in my veins, throbbing and pulsing. I take a breath and swallow, hiding beneath the shelter of a live oak. Under the tree, I hold on to the skirt of my gown long enough to spot dirty stains along the hemline. Before, the dress was soft and silky, unblemished and white.

*Wedding white.*

"Just say it!" the same voice hisses. "You killed her!"

Something tugs at my heart, as if a string were attached that someone just pulled too tight. Moistening my lower lip, I check my surroundings and watch my breath. I'm shivering and shaking, chilled to the bone from the stinging cold. But I keep going.

There is a river up ahead. I hear it from a distance and see the rushing water once I approach the bank. With every step I take, the temperature drops one degree lower. My teeth are chattering by the time I see him. But his back is to me. Nothing is clear.

I try to reach him, but the woods obscure my path. So I trample through the wilderness and dodge low-hanging limbs. An owl flies overhead with a large enough wingspan to make me shriek. And by the time I catch my breath, I freeze at the sound of a gunshot.

My heart thuds at the base of my throat as I wait for a sign. Someone is dead.

Beyond my wit's end, I cut through the trees and emerge into a pool of moonlight. He sees me and comes over, hanging his head on my chest. "I'm sorry," he cries. He looks back and whispers, "I didn't mean to do it."

"Tony." I touch his back as his breath lingers

on my arm. "I think you should go."

Nodding, he sniffles and sobs, hugging me one last time. The gun slips from his hand, and I catch it with mine. With his body pressed against me, blood clings to my pretty white dress.

"You were always my favorite," he confesses. "You were the one."

As I pull away, he clamps his large hands around my waist. "Tony, let me go."

"I can't," he sobs, his hot breath searing down my neck. "I won't."

Fluttering my lashes, I look up and ask, "Why not?"

Tony leans closer and whispers in my ear, "Because you know my secret."

I lose my nerve and drop the gun, tempted to peer over his shoulder. "I'm scared," I whisper back, quivering at the mere thought of what he has done.

"Why don't you go have a look?" he encourages. "See what you've done."

My brow furrows in confusion. What *I've* done? I don't want to know.

"Go on!" he shouts, egging me on.

He pushes me towards the river and then kicks me in the back when I don't move fast enough. Falling forward, I brace myself in time to land on my hands and knees. The water meets my fingertips, as I struggle for air. I've had the wind knocked out of me.

"Look!" He pulls my hair and my head snaps

back. "Look at her!"

My lower lip trembles while tears stream down from my eyes. I don't want to look. I don't want to see. Because I know Antoinette's body is the one floating in the river.

Her feet are bare, and her pretty white dress is covered in blood. I smell salt and rust, retreating from the pungent odor. I think I'm going to be sick.

"Don't be a coward!" he booms. "Do it!"

When he pushes me again, I land in the water. I cough and gag, up to my elbows in the river stench. My dress is soaking wet, but I can't bring myself to study the look on her face.

Tired of waiting, he stands behind me and grabs my head, jerking my chin towards Antoinette. But when I see the dead body, panic sets in. I jump and scream, bucking against him as he covers my mouth.

Despite my agony, he holds my head above water. Then he sets his chin on my shoulder and talks to me, running his knuckles down my cheek. When I see his reflection in the river, he snakes his arm around my waist so there is no opportunity for me to flee.

"You're mine now," he whispers, soft yet possessive. "You've always belonged to me."

As his fingers traipse down my throat, I stare into his amber eyes and freeze.

The man holding my body is Ricky.

And the dead lady in the river is me.

# Chapter 1

I sprang awake in bed like a gun went off.

Lightning flashed into my room as thunder shook the house, rain pelting hard and heavy against the glass. I sat up and pushed the covers back, threading my fingers through my hair. My knees went into my chest as I struggled to catch my breath, still reeling from the nightmare.

Once I recovered, sweat dotted my upper neck and back. I slipped out of bed and trudged into the bathroom, splashing cool water on my face. When I looked in the mirror, my eyes hardly had time to adjust. So I pulled away, unwilling to trust the glass just yet.

Rocking back on my heels, I put my hands on my hips and walked back into my bedroom. Tonight was a rare one with Jeffrey and Eleanor asleep downstairs. Usually, they were so consumed with work—Eleanor a doctor and Jeffrey a lawyer—

that they spent the night in town, if they weren't traveling that is.

But their presence never made me feel safe or loved.

In fact, after a nightmare as bad as that one, all I really felt was alone.

After pacing the floor for a few minutes, I opened the closet and took off my clothes. As I was changing into a sports bra and shorts, I paid careful attention to my rapid breathing. Nearly a month and I still couldn't get over it. I couldn't escape what had happened that night.

I slipped into a pair of running shoes and pulled the laces tight, even when it made my feet throb. Then I grabbed a black jacket and tugged my arms through the sleeves. The house creaked and I spun around fast, feeling my heart make its way up my throat.

I had to get out of here.

Despite the heavy downpour, I opened my bedroom window and climbed onto the tree outside. Thunder sounded right in my ear, as I leaned back to shut the window. I dodged the rain and pulled my hood up over my head, slowly scaling my way down the trunk. The bark was wet and slippery, so I nearly fell to my death a handful of times.

Once I landed on the ground, I zipped my jacket up and took off running. I sloshed through mud puddles as I made my way through the forest. But I kept on. Even when the thunder and lightning made me shiver.

My breathing was heavy by the time I reached the fence separating our land. I looked over my shoulder and then turned around to make sure no one was watching me. Ever since prom night, it always felt like someone was.

With my heart pounding, I climbed the fence and hopped over to Sutton territory. Then I ran the rest of the way without looking back.

When the mansion came into view, I slowed down and put my hands on my hips. As I walked around the side of the house, I saw a light on in Tom's bedroom and breathed a sigh of relief. He was up, too. But maybe it wasn't just the rain keeping him awake.

Maybe he couldn't sleep either.

I had just sought shelter beneath the trees when he turned his light out. So I grabbed a handful of rocks and tossed the first one at his window. Even though summer was near, I was cold and wet out here in the rain.

Relentless, I tossed a few more rocks until he came to the window and opened it.

"What are you doing?" Tom leaned against the sill, while I admired the view. He was tall, tan, and fit with a chiseled jawline and washboard abs. He also wasn't wearing a shirt.

I tilted my head back and smirked up at him. "I can't sleep."

"Then why didn't you just come in?" he pointed out. "You have a key."

"Yeah," I agreed, staring up at him. "But this is more fun."

Tom chuckled and shook his head from side to side. Then he gestured towards me. "Come on up then."

Brimming with anticipation, I bit my lip and smiled. There was an oak tree standing behind me, right outside his bedroom window. I had never climbed it before, but for the first time, I was about to try.

"What's takin' you so long?" Tom peered down at me, laying on the Southern charm.

Not afraid of a challenge, I hoisted myself onto the lowest limb and then planted my foot in a groove within the heart of the tree. Rain continued to pour as the wind whipped in my face, blowing leaves and branches against my body. As I worked my way up, a strip of bark left a scrape on my knee and I winced at the burning sensation.

When I reached the top, Tom leaned through the window. But the thunder startled me and I lost my footing, grasping for his arm. "Tom!"

He put his hands under my arms and pulled me towards the window, as I slipped from the tree. My eyes landed on the steep drop below, where I imagined collapsing to a tragic death. All because I wanted to climb through my boyfriend's second story window.

"Come on!" he encouraged, yelling over the storm. "I've got you."

My hands settled at the back of his neck as

Tom grabbed my waist. When my upper torso was through the opening, he picked me up in his arms and pulled me the rest of the way. Tom stepped backwards into his bedroom, and we collapsed on the floor.

"Ah," Tom gasped. I knew that he had taken the brunt of the fall.

"I'm so sorry, baby." I got on my knees and sat back. "Are you okay?"

Tom lifted his head and looked up to see that I was safe. "Yeah," he muttered. "I'm fine."

Happy to have him near, I leaned down and kissed him. Tom stilled beneath me, shutting his eyes to absorb the feeling. He wasn't expecting that.

When he revealed those golden eyes, I lay down on top of him and put my head on his chest. Tom rubbed my back and held me in his arms, probably wondering why I was acting like a child. But I just wanted to feel close to someone.

I wanted to be touched. I wanted to be held.

"Addie," Tom murmured beneath me, his firm hand against my back.

"Yes." I buried my head in his warmth, comfortable and protected.

"This is great, but I need to close the window."

"Oh." I looked back and saw the rain pouring in. "Right."

Tom smiled as I helped him up, but a sudden flush of heat came over me that I couldn't explain. By the time he shut the window, my cheeks were burning red.

I braided my fingers together and watched him in the night. The way his skin glimmered beneath each shock of lightning. There was tension in his body. Cuts of muscle. Veins in his arms. He was strong and beautiful. And he was also *mine.*

Feeling my eyes on him, Tom turned back and snickered. "See somethin' you like?"

"Shut up," I sassed, narrowing my gaze. He watched me approach him and then took my hand once I reached the window. My clothes were dripping wet, but I hadn't noticed.

Tom eyed me up and down with the lick of his lips, but there was something innocent about it. Like he was looking for the truth of the matter— what was I really doing here?

As I stood with my back to the window, Tom knelt down and untied my shoelaces. He flicked those eyes up at me for just a moment. They were the color of honey.

I held on to his shoulders as he slipped my foot out of one shoe and then the other. When my feet touched the carpet, Tom pushed my shoes aside. Then he slowly rose from the ground, eyeing every inch of my figure along the way.

Breathless, I felt that searing heat return— though it never really left—as he branded every part of me with just a look. Tom blinked a few times and then gazed into my eyes, pushing the hood of my jacket off my head. I longed for his touch and thought he might caress my face. But his hands moved to my jacket instead, where he began tugging the zipper down.

"What's on your mind?" he whispered, exposing my sports bra and then my bare stomach beneath it. He pressed a gentle kiss into my forehead as my eyelids fluttered. His body heat was all around me, enveloping me like a winter cloak.

"Umm..." I lost my train of thought, distracted by his scent.

"Addie." He dragged the pad of his thumb across my cheek. "What is it?"

When he lifted my chin, I looked up at him and sighed. His golden eyes were on me, burning right through my self-control. I put my hand on his chest and studied his lips.

Tom cupped my cheek in his hand as our torsos became flush. "Well?"

Pulsing with excitement, I leaned in and sealed my mouth over his. Tom froze as I curled my fingers around his back, deepening the kiss. When his hands slid down to my waist, I felt the pressure of his palms against my bare skin.

He touched his nose to mine, and our breaths rivaled in the night.

It had been four months since we met, but it felt like I had known him a lifetime. I loved him, trusted him. And I wanted to be closer. I wanted to be *his*.

Since Daniel's death, we were the only thing each other had to hold on to. But I wasn't just holding on. I was clinging to the sweet solace I had found in his arms. With parents who could care less about my well-being, it was no wonder we had found each other.

My parents were really *adoptive* parents, *legal* guardians. And Tom was an orphan. Daniel was the only family either of us ever had. Daniel had been Tom's godfather and my biological grandfather. After his death, I worried that Tom and I might fall apart.

His chest rose and fell, while I waited for him to make the next move. I moistened my lower lip and gasped when he squeezed my body in his arms. Tom molded his mouth to mine and traced the edge of my jaw with his thumb, forcing my knees to buckle.

When I fell forward, Tom took on the full weight of my body. I whimpered at the heavenly dose of kisses, running my nails along the side of his arm. As his lips returned to mine, I sank into his embrace and we somehow ended up on the bed.

Tom wrapped me in his arms while we wrestled with the sheets, two kids crazy in love. Looking back now, we were young and vulnerable, only seventeen. Neither of us willing to acknowledge the raging hormones driving our passion, our aggression.

I just wanted to be loved. And I wanted Tom to be the one to do it.

"Addie," Tom rasped, his breath in my ear.

"Addie, wait a minute."

He held himself above me as I stared up at him, my head on his pillow. My eyes darted across his face, searching for signs of what I had done wrong. He almost looked scared.

"Hey." I sat up and stroked the stubble on his face. "What is it?"

Tom knelt down on the mattress and looked away, running his hand over his mouth.

"Hey," I repeated. "What is it?"

But Tom stared at the sheet and threaded his fingers through his hair.

"Talk to me," I begged. "Tell me what's going on."

In recent weeks, things between us hadn't been the same. We were on different wave lengths. He didn't open up to me. He didn't share. Some days, it felt like I didn't even know him anymore. And I wanted to. I wanted to know him all over again.

When he dared to look at me, Tom turned around and leaned against his pillow with a sigh. Curling closer, I put my head on his shoulder and touched his arm. He was so warm.

"I'm sorry," he whispered, showing me the guilt in his eyes.

"It's okay." I hung my head and let go of his arm. My spirit was gone.

"No, it's not." Tom turned my cheek into the palm of his hand.

I looked down and tried to feel anything besides disappointment. "What did I do wrong?"

"Nothing." He placed his hands on my shoulders. "You did nothing wrong."

"Then why won't you—?" I set my green gaze on him, but it was no use tonight.

"Look, Addie, I'm a mess right now. Up here." He tapped two fingers against his temple. "I'm still in shock. I come home to this empty house and Grandpa's not here." He looked around the room and let go of me, lost in another world, one that I didn't have access to. "I know things aren't the best with your parents, but at least you have them."

It took all I could not to roll my eyes at the mention of Jeffrey and Eleanor.

Tom stared at the wall as his voice began to shake. "I've got no one."

"That's not true." I wrapped my hand around his arm. "You've got me."

Sighing aloud, Tom looked over me with a barely there smile. When our eyes met, he lifted his hand to cup my cheek. I reveled in the comfort of his caress, nuzzling closer.

But then he hesitated and pulled away. "You should get some sleep."

I lowered my head with a reluctant nod, tucking my hair behind my ears. "Okay."

Even though I understood his pain, every bit of it seemed to be at my expense. Maybe he was hurting. But I was hurting, too. What about the way I felt?

I *needed* him.

"Do you mind if I stay?" I searched his eyes,

but he wasn't looking at me anymore.

Tom shook his head and got out of bed, trudging towards the door.

"Where are you going?" I whined, longing for his warmth in the night.

"I can't sleep," he grumbled.

"Okay." I sat up and patted the spot beside me. "Then why don't we talk?"

"No." He shook his head again, threading his fingers through his hair. "You're tired." As he rubbed his eyes, I wondered why he was avoiding me. "Just go to bed, Addie."

When he walked off and headed downstairs, I was surprised that he even left the door open. It felt like he was keeping secrets from me. I had no idea what they were.

Utterly defeated, I lay down and pulled the covers on top of me. Then I rolled onto my side and huffed, watching the rain through the window. The whole reason I came over was because I couldn't sleep alone in my bedroom. Now I was sleeping alone in his.

Tom thought he had insomnia. But mine was the induced kind. I hated falling asleep, because I never knew when the next nightmare would come. They were hard to take.

Sometimes, it felt like I was trapped inside a glass box filled with too much water or not enough air. I could drown. I could suffocate. And then there were the dreams about Ricky. Or even worse, DeMilo. I couldn't get them out of my head. I wanted it to stop.

Nestling beneath the covers, I grabbed Tom's pillow and hugged it close. I would much rather be squeezing him tight. But that was hard to do when he disappeared all the time.

I cried alone in the dark. He made me feel unwanted. He had rejected me.

Exhausted, I shut my eyes and inhaled his scent. Then I felt a pair of arms wrap around me. "I'm sorry," he whispered in my ear, his breath cascading down my neck.

I touched his hand, and it felt rough. Rougher than usual.

When I looked over my shoulder, he was gone. Jerking up in bed, I pulled the covers back. But no one was there. I patted the spot beside me, and it didn't even feel warm.

With my heart racing, I got out of bed and approached the door.

There was no one in the room but me.

Barreling down the staircase, I darted through the house in search of Tom. He wasn't in the kitchen or dining room. Panic set in, as I felt blood pumping through my veins.

"Tom," I cried, trying to keep my voice down. "Tom."

All of the blinds were drawn, and the fireplace was flickering way too fast. Almost like someone was blowing air over the flames.

"Tom?" I stepped into the hallway. Every door was open except for the one leading to Daniel's room. "Tom?" I gasped, hearing the break in my voice.

I looked back over my shoulder.

It felt like someone was watching me.

I couldn't breathe.

"Tom?" I knocked on the door. "Tom, are you in there?"

When there was no reply, I twisted the knob and let myself inside. It was so dark in the bedroom, that I couldn't even see my hands. I bumped up against something, and it hurt.

"Tom!" I hissed. "Tom, where are you?"

As lightning flashed in the night sky, I looked out the window and screamed.

DeMilo was standing outside in the rain.

## Chapter 2

I shot up out of bed dripping in sweat. Tom ran into the room as I came back to reality, struggling to catch my breath. Everything around me was spinning. I felt dizzy, tipsy.

"Hey, hey, hey." Tom put his hand on my shoulder. "You're okay."

"Tom, I don't feel good." I looked down and listened to the pulsing in my ears.

"Addie, look at me." He tugged at my chin. "You're okay. Breathe. You're fine."

I shut my eyes and took deep breaths, but the feeling wouldn't go away.

"I feel like I'm gonna be sick," I confessed, pressing my hand to my stomach.

"What?" Tom stroked his fingers through my hair. "Addie."

I shoved past him and sprinted into the bathroom. Then I leaned over the toilet and puked for no apparent reason. Relief immediately kicked in, and I sat back against the wall.

Tom knelt down in front of me with a damp washcloth. "Why didn't you tell me they were getting this bad?" As he wiped my face, I reached over to flush the toilet. Then I put the lid down and rested against the wall. "Addie, your nightmares, I didn't realize—"

"I'm fine." I snatched the washcloth out of his hand and stood up.

After getting so sick, I probably should have been taking it slow. But I was mad at him. The nightmares weren't bad. They were awful. I came here to make them go away.

But Tom left me alone in the dark. Like a child without a night light.

I didn't want to sleep by myself tonight. If I had known he was going to make me, I never would have come. I could wake up sweating and get sick at my own house.

Tom sat down on the toilet and sighed, rubbing the back of his neck. I approached the sink and rinsed my face off with cool water. Then I tossed the washcloth on the counter and opened the medicine cabinet for my toothbrush.

"I should have stayed with you tonight," Tom said. "I'm sorry I left you alone."

Ignoring him, I stared in the mirror and brushed my teeth. I was hot with malice, because the whole nightmare could have been avoided. If only he had stayed with me.

I rinsed my mouth out and put my toothbrush away, wondering why I even kept one over here. There was no need to come over if I was still going to end up sleeping alone.

"Maybe I should just go home," I suggested.

"What?" Tom rose to his feet.

I had his attention now.

"Why? You just got sick." He reached out to me and I pulled away, retreating into the bedroom. "Addie, look, I'm sorry I left. All right? Please don't stay mad at me forever."

"Why would I do that?" I countered. "Isn't that your job?"

He leaned against the wall with a grunt, crossing his arms over his chest.

"What? Am I being too honest?" I turned back and stared into his golden eyes.

"That's not fair." He shook his head. "I've never been mad at you like that."

"Then why are you punishing me?" I stood on the other side of the bed.

Tom took several steps towards me. "I'm not," he whispered.

"I really needed you tonight," I confessed, baring my soul. "I thought I would sleep better in your arms." I side stepped him when he tried to touch me. "But you didn't care."

Tom pursed his lips but didn't say anything.

"I know how messed up you are right now, because I'm messed up, too!" I jabbed my finger in his chest, and his jaw tightened. "But you can't keep pushing me away!"

Right then and there, I broke down and started crying. It was all too much.

DeMilo. Ricky. Daniel.

It had been a month, and I didn't know how to handle it.

When I dropped down to my knees, all the air went out of my lungs. I put my forehead on the mattress and held on, trying to keep my body from falling over. Tom sat down beside me and rubbed my back, eventually pulling me into his arms.

As he cradled my head against his chest, I wrapped my arms around his waist and squeezed so tight that he winced. Letting up, I mumbled an apology into his t-shirt and then curled deeper into his body. Tom turned my chin up in the palm of his hand.

"Do you want to know the real reason why I've been distant?"

Sniffling, I gazed into his eyes and nodded.

Tom dragged the back of his knuckles down my arm. "I'm scared."

Clinging to his shirt, I tilted my head back and asked, "Of what?"

He stared into my eyes without blinking. "You."

"What?" It was so silly I almost wanted to laugh. "Why?"

"I'm scared I won't be able to take my hands off of you." He held my body closer and smoothed his thumb across my cheek. "I'm scared

I won't be able to stop."

Desire thrummed through me at the thought. I took his hand and moved it to the small of my back, dissolving the space between us. "What if I don't want you to?"

Tom shut his eyes and swallowed. "You really shouldn't say things like that to me."

I looked down, and his gaze pierced right through me. Then I took his hand and folded his fingers through mine. It was bare flesh. Skin-to-skin. Palm-to-palm.

"You're the only thing I have left to care about," I whispered in the dark.

Maybe I was trying to be seductive. Maybe I was just being honest.

"I love you." I touched the side of his face with my hand, and Tom turned into my touch. His cheek was rough, covered in stubble. But I liked the way it felt.

"I love you, too." He watched me through those long black lashes, his eyes like warm golden honey. His fingers crept down the side of my neck, long and deft. Every breath from his lips sent tingles down my spine. With each passing second, the feeling amplified.

Slowly melting, I bit my lip and tugged at the collar of his shirt. His eyes dropped to my mouth, and I wanted to sing the Hallelujah Chorus. As he came closer, I felt that burning ache spread through me, scorching my skin. Like a need I couldn't suppress without him.

When our lips met, I dug my nails into the back of his neck and clung to the sensation. His fingertips swept across my spine, but there was resistance on his end. So I curled my arms around him until my stomach grazed his, and we were sitting chest to chest.

Tom leaned back and cupped my cheek in his hand. "I don't want to rush you."

Gasping for breath, I brushed my lips against his and whispered, "You're not."

I felt the smile on his face and settled in his lap, sliding my fingers beneath his shirt. Tom tensed up at the intimate contact, so I let my hand go. His arms tightened around my waist, as I adjusted to the feel of him all around me. Breathless and close—like we used to be before DeMilo came into the picture and ruined everything.

Surrendering to the moment, I curled my arms around his neck and swooned. It was something Tom hadn't let me do in a long time. I felt at peace in his arms. Safe. Like I had finally found my home. But there was so much distance between us. So much we had to work through. Sometimes it felt like mistrust instead.

As we kissed, all it took was one touch to change everything. Tom dipped his head and pressed a kiss into my neck. I shut my eyes and sighed, absorbing the pleasure. When his lips traveled lower, I put my hand on his shoulder and dug my fingers in his hair.

"Addie." Tom brought me back down to earth with the touch of his hand. His eyes dropped to my mouth, and I wondered if I had won.

Was he finally going to give me what I wanted?

"Tom," I whimpered.

We looked at each other for a few seconds, but it felt like minutes. My heart was beating so fast. It was like he had a direct line to my bloodstream. He was in my veins.

"Okay," he finally said, touching his nose to mine. "Okay."

It took a while for his words to resonate. I tilted my head to the side and traced the edge of his jawline, noticing the way his chest rose and fell. "Tom, I don't want to—"

"No." He shook his head, grasping my face to pull me back in. "It's okay." His Adam's apple bobbed as I looked into his eyes. "I've wanted this for a long time. I've wanted you."

Lowering my lashes, I felt the blood pumping as my cheeks flushed with pink. But then I gazed up at him and tried to be brazen, playing it cool. "Then what are we waiting for?"

Tom hesitated, those amber eyes shifting over every inch of my face. "You're sure about this?" His thumb slipped down the hollow of my neck, which made it hard to breathe.

"Yeah," I rasped. "Yeah, I'm sure."

And I was sure. I'd thought about it for weeks. Meeting Tom was the best thing that ever happened to me. There was no doubt in my mind that he didn't feel the same way.

But it was more than that—my desire to be his.

We loved each other.

It was first love, young love, whatever you want to call it. But not the kind that ends in bitter disdain or teen pregnancy. This was a forever kind of thing.

And I know how naïve that must sound. Especially coming from a girl like me—as inexperienced as they come. But nothing about our relationship was stereotypical.

We weren't an ordinary couple.

Our fates were inevitably entwined. And Daniel had been the single piece of thread. The loved one who brought us together in life and death.

As irresponsible as Jeffrey and Eleanor were, I had to thank them for the neglect. Their absence had opened up a door and let Tom in. The ironic bit was the fact that he had been there all along, silently watching and waiting.

It was only a matter of time before the two of us got together.

It was written in the stars. Fate. Destiny.

I didn't want to change any of it. Because being with Tom felt like a choice. Not some stroke of bad luck or ill fortune. I *wanted* to be with him. Now and then.

And there was nothing anybody could do to change that.

"Are you okay?" I whispered, stroking his

cheek with my hand.

Tom swallowed and licked his lips. "My heart is beating so fast."

I touched my forehead to his and placed his hand over my heart. "So is mine."

"And you really want to do this?" He tucked a lock of hair behind my ear.

"Yeah," I consented. "I really do. I've given it a lot of thought."

"You have?" He rubbed my arm, and I could tell how nervous he was.

"Yeah." I forced a little smile, leaning in closer. "I want all of you."

On that note, Tom pulled me in from the back of my neck and sealed his mouth over mine. We kissed as my hand slipped beneath his shirt again, this time tracing his spine. Tom leaned back and pulled his shirt over his head, tossing it to the way side and reaching for me instead.

When my palm settled on his warm skin, I knew that this was what I wanted. Everything about being with him felt right. And there was no turning back now.

He pushed my hair over my shoulders and molded his mouth with mine. My eyes slid closed, as I got lost in the sensation. We were all out of air, and the night hadn't even started.

Tom stood up and grabbed my hand, jerking me to my feet. Our torsos were flush, and every part of me was buzzing with anticipation. An ache had coursed through me, resonating in my belly and burning beneath my skin. It was almost unbearable.

"Where do you want to do this?" He grasped my chin and stared.

The corner of my mouth lifted into a smile. "How about your bed?"

"Oh." He kissed me again. "I guess that's pretty obvious."

When he pulled away, I bit my lip so I wouldn't laugh. He took my hand and folded his fingers through mine, leading me around to his side of the bed. Then he pulled the covers back and invited me to climb beneath them, following closely behind.

"What would your parents say if they knew what we were about to do?"

I thought about it for a second and then decided, "Use protection."

Tom laughed, and I was so thankful for it. We needed something to lighten the mood. As nervous as I felt, I wondered if it was worse for him somehow. He was a decent guy.

I sat beside him and put my hand over his heart. He placed his hand over mine and then wrapped the other around my back. His breath felt like a feather against my skin.

"I don't wanna screw this up," he confessed. "I only get one chance to do this right."

I kissed him on the cheek, and the space between us evaporated. "You won't."

Just like that, Tom relaxed and took control. I

breathed an internal sigh of relief.

His fingers tangled through my hair as my head dropped to the pillow. I curled my hands around his back and closed my eyes, relishing every kiss. His lips forged a path down my neck, while my lashes fluttered to the rhythm of my heartbeat.

"I don't want to hurt you." He pushed up on his hands, hovering above me.

Sensing his unease, I tugged at the nape of his neck and whispered, "You won't." Tom furrowed his brow, struggling to return his mouth to mine. "You won't," I promised.

Tom leaned back on his elbow as I slid out from underneath him. "I'm sorry." He rubbed his hand over his face, catching his breath. "I've never done this before."

"I know," I whispered, tugging my sports bra over my head. "Neither have I."

His hand pressed into my back as I lay against him, delivering the next kiss. When his fingertips traipsed my spine, I curved my body into his and shuddered.

"You're so beautiful," he said, laying me on the flat of my back.

I looked up at him and combed my fingers through his hair. "So are you."

Tom kissed the end of my nose and then planted his lips on my cheek.

Growing impatient, I forced him closer until his mouth landed on mine. Fire burned through me, scorching my veins after everything he touched. I wrapped my body around his, wanton and desperate for him to give me what I wanted.

As he crushed his lips to mine, someone pounded on the front door.

"Tom," I gasped, breaking the kiss. "Who is that?"

He lifted his head and listened, stilling above me.

There was silence. And then that thumping loud rap against the door.

"Tom," I hissed. He held a finger to his lips and climbed out of bed.

As he approached the bedroom door, I sat up with the sheet covering me.

You could hear a pin drop until they banged on the front door again, whoever they were.

"Tom," I panicked, watching him cross the threshold.

He turned around and picked up his t-shirt, tossing it at me. "Put this on."

I slipped my arms through the sleeves and tugged the shirt down over me.

He squeezed my hand and left a kiss on my forehead. "I'll be right back."

"No." I grabbed his arm. "Don't leave me."

"Addie, let go," he growled. "I'll be right back."

I loosened my hold as he pulled away and disappeared into the hall.

For two minutes, I stayed in his room pacing the floor. But then I couldn't take it anymore—not knowing if he was okay, wondering if he was dead or alive.

So I disregarded his warning and slipped into the hallway. Darkness surrounded me, nearly swallowing me whole as I crept down the staircase. Once I reached the bottom, there was no sign of a visitor. The banging on the door had stopped.

I turned left and tiptoed into the kitchen, on the hunt for Tom.

But he wasn't there.

As I entered the den, a flicker of light caught my eye. I moved closer to investigate until someone grabbed me from behind.

I fought and bucked against him—the tall man taking me down. But he was too strong, clamping his hand over my mouth before I had the chance to scream. He pinned my back to his chest and crouched down, sitting against the wall with me in his grasp.

"Shh," Tom hissed. "It's me."

Breathing a sigh of relief, I leaned my head on his chest and relaxed.

But then I heard footsteps, and a flashlight bounced against the window.

"Someone's outside," Tom whispered, leaving his hand over my mouth.

We heard hushed voices, as men barked at each other on the porch.

"How many are there?" Tom asked. "Listen, Addie. Listen."

I shut my eyes and held on to Tom. But it was

hard to make out.

Pounding footsteps. Car doors slamming. An engine starting.

We waited until they left. And once they were gone, I panicked.

"Come here." Tom turned me into his arms so we were face to face.

I nuzzled his chest and breathed in his scent, thankful when he held me tight.

"How many voices did you count? I think I heard three."

"Yeah," I nodded. "Three."

Tom stood up and peeked out the window to make sure they were gone.

"What is it?" I pulled my knees into my chest, while my heart kept on pounding.

"I think I see something," he said, toying with the blinds.

"What?" I snapped. "What do you see?"

"I don't know." He stepped away from the window. "I'm going outside to check."

No. That was the last thing I wanted. After everything we had been through, Tom should have known better than to walk out on the front porch in the middle of the night. What if they were still there? Just hiding in the bushes?

It wasn't like it hadn't happened before.

"Wait." I leapt to my feet and grabbed his arm. "Don't go out there. Not yet."

"Addie, I have to go out there some time." Searching my face, he touched my shoulders and sighed. "I'll be fine. Just trust me. Okay?"

I nodded, but not before diving back into his arms.

Tom rubbed my back and sighed. "They're gone. I promise."

"Enough to let me go out there with you?"

He huffed in response. "Okay. But let me walk out there first."

I hugged him close and refused to let go. But then he pulled back and planted a kiss on my forehead. As he turned to leave, I grabbed his wrist and slanted my lips over his. Tom lingered for a moment, sliding his fingers through my golden hair.

"I'm sure it's nothing," he decided. "Everything is going to be all right."

I followed at his heels and whimpered, "You promise?"

He glanced back at me with a frown that told me he wasn't so sure.

As he opened the door, I stayed back and listened for any sign that they were still there. We were known for conjuring uninvited guests. Unwillingly or not, it just happened.

Tom stepped on the front porch and looked out into the wilderness. Once he felt safe, I slipped out after him and leaned against the house. There was a note pinned to a wooden post, blowing in the wind. He reached out to grab it, and I turned ice cold.

"What does it say?" I stared at his back, hating

the suspense.

Tom read the note and froze.

The storm had calmed down for the night. But soft rain blew across the porch, littering my face with dew. I would have welcomed the cool moisture, if not for my racing heart.

"Tom?"

He lifted his head and turned around, sharing a cursory glance with me. I pulled my brows together with worry as he approached. When he handed me the note, I almost didn't want to read it. But I bit the bullet and looked anyway. Because I knew I had to.

Three words. As familiar to me as the color of Tom's eyes. And just as hypnotic.

*Find the necklace.*

Only this time, they were written in blood.

All of the air left my lungs, and I forgot how to breathe.

Tom stared at me, and we both knew.

It was happening again.

# Chapter 3

I left my thoughts on the porch, and that was where they stayed. When Tom drove me to school, I figured he must have been contemplating much of the same. We hadn't spoken about what happened last night. After I read the note, he sealed it in a Ziploc bag and wondered if we shouldn't have gotten our fingerprints all over it.

Riding shotgun, I leaned my head against the window and drifted off. Tom put his hand on my knee, as a thrill of passion raced through me. Despite our failed attempt at intimacy, I felt like the previous night wasn't a total bust. We were in love, and when it came to making love, we would get there soon enough.

It was Friday—the last day of school.

Over the past semester, so much of my life had changed. My new friendship with Jeanine, falling in love with Tom, tolerating Nicki, and watching

Ricky die. Since prom, Maple Creek High hadn't felt the same. If only it were my senior year coming to an end.

I couldn't wait to be out of here for good.

"Hey!" Jeanine crooned, sliding up beside me. "Already clean your locker out?"

"Yeah," I answered. "There's not much left since exams are done."

"I know, I can't wait to see how I did."

"Yeah, me too." I opened my locker to clear out what was left.

"Are you okay?" Jeanine was wearing heavy mascara. It made her blue eyes pop.

"Yeah, I'm fine. Just tired is all." I tossed out some scratch paper and zipped my backpack up, leaving my locker for whoever might get it next semester.

"Thank God it's only a half day." Tom snuck up behind me and kissed my cheek.

Jeanine narrowed her eyes, that black bob bouncing with every motion.

"What?" Tom leaned against the lockers but stayed close to me.

"You're acting strange," she suspected. "Both of you."

"It's nothing," I clipped. "Just sick of all this studying and glad it's over."

When I forced a smile, she bought it. But Jeanine was smarter than I gave her credit for. She was intuitive, and she must have sensed the slight wall that had formed between us. The Ricky factor was bound to cause some strain, because how could it not?

He almost raped me, and now he was dead.

And Jeanine was his little sister.

"Have y'all seen Nicki lately?" she asked. I was thankful for the subject change.

"No. I don't think so. Not since before finals week. Why? Where has she been?"

"I don't know," she whispered. "But I heard Principal Caldwell let her exempt all of her finals. So unfair, right?"

Maple Creek High didn't allow students to exempt final exams. With the exception of extreme circumstances, that is. Like your father being the guy who runs the place.

"Yeah, but why are you surprised?" Tom noted. "He lets her get away with everything."

Nicki entered the double doors and everyone stared. She must have been gone for two weeks. Maybe not consecutively, but when you added up all the sick days, two weeks.

Audible gasps ignited in the hallway.

During her absence, Nicki had become unrecognizable.

Her face was pale white and utterly bare—without a drop of makeup. I had never seen her without some sort of cosmetic enhancement. She had lost a considerable amount of weight since Ricky's death, maybe as much as twenty pounds.

There was a time when Nicki looked healthy and thin. And she had dressed the part to show it.

But now she wore a pair of tattered blue jeans that hung loosely on her hips, too baggy to fit her shrinking body. She was scrawny and weak, lacking color.

Even her signature cork-screw curls lay brittle and flat, like pieces of straw used to stuff a scarecrow. I hated to admit it, but Nicki was a washed out version of her former self.

She looked like a ghost.

The bell rang as students scrambled, rushing off to their last day of class. Jeanine headed upstairs and Tom tugged at my elbow, encouraging me to follow his lead.

"You go ahead," I said. "I'll be there in a minute."

Tom noticed Nicki alone in the hall and then set his sights on me.

"I want to talk to her," I hissed, wishing he would go so I could.

"Why?" He looked me in the eye, unable to understand.

"Because she's going through a lot right now. I want to see if she's okay."

Tom shook his head and sighed. "God, you must be a saint."

"Thank you." We kissed and he walked off, leaving me alone with Nicki.

All was silent as she stood in front of her locker. I looked around to make sure no one was watching us. Even though I had no idea what to say, I walked up to her with the best of intentions.

We had all been through a lot. Jeanine and Tom included. Ricky's death had affected everyone, so we should have been working through it together. Not letting it keep us apart.

"Hey, Nicki." I stood beside her, noting her gaunt, angular frame. She was wearing a black sweater, which was odd considering the ninety degree weather.

"What do you want, Addie?" Her tone was dismissive, intended to blow me off.

"I just wanted to see how you were doing. We've been wondering where you were."

Nicki slammed her locker shut and clutched the purse over her shoulder. It was the only thing left of the Barbie doll she used to be. "You've never liked me. Neither has Jeanine or your stupid boyfriend. Don't act like you care now."

"I'm sorry. I just thought you might want to talk to someone about—"

"I don't *need* to talk to anyone! I'm fine!" Her eyes were tired and black.

"You don't look fine." Maybe I shouldn't have been so blunt. But it was the truth.

"You think I don't already know that?" She glared in an attempt to run me off.

"We've all been a little messed up after what happened to Ricky. I just thought—"

"Is that what this is about? You didn't know him like I did, okay?"

Biting my tongue, I shut up for a second and looked away. "I know you loved him."

She lifted her head, and I noticed the dark circles under her eyes.

"But Jeanine loved him, too," I reminded her.

"It's not the same. She doesn't know him like I do. None of you know him like I do!"

"Nicki, I will never understand what the two of you had. But I'm trying to help."

"You wish you did." She got in my face, backing me up against the lockers. "I saw the way you used to look at him. Whatever he was going to do to you that night, you wanted it."

It took all I could not to cry in front of her. But I swallowed the lump in my throat and tried to put myself in her shoes. There is no telling what Ricky might have done to her.

"I'm sorry."

She tied her hair back in a loose ponytail as her shirtsleeve rode up. My eyes flicked to the marks on her wrist, and she noticed before I could look away.

"Nicki," I murmured, sympathizing with her situation.

"It's my life." She pulled her sleeve back down to conceal her wrist. "Stay out of it."

I watched her storm off and bust through the double doors. A tear trickled down my cheek, and I hurried to wipe it away. That was one of the last times I ever saw her.

When I made it to class, our teacher ignored my tardiness. Since finals were over, today had technically been optional. But most of us were required to attend anyway.

I took a seat beside Tom in the back and put my head on my desk. All the lights were off, because they were showing a movie in class today. *The Old Man and the Sea* or something like that. I didn't care, because I couldn't get those marks out of my head.

Tom watched me until I felt him staring. "You okay?" he mouthed.

Scanning the room, I looked back at him and said, "I'll tell you later."

The half-day dragged on for what felt like weeks. I was so glad when the bell finally rang and I could leave. I had no intention of staying for lunch or asking anyone to sign my yearbook. I just wanted to get out of there. Even though Nicki had already disappeared.

"Why don't we go out to eat? School's out! We should celebrate! My treat." Jeanine waved her wallet in the back seat, as I looked in the rearview mirror.

Tom turned to me and shrugged. "Well, what do you think?"

"I'm feeling kind of tired," I said. "I'd rather just go home."

"Okay, well, we have all summer to hang out I guess," Jeanine accepted.

"Maybe some other time." Tom turned back and smiled at her.

I hoped that made her feel better, because I was feeling god awful.

Jeanine talked all the way to Chateau Rogue. I hardly heard a word she said. But when she got out, I thought I remembered her saying something about Leonardo DiCaprio. She was having a movie marathon tonight in his honor. It was nice to know that some things hadn't changed.

"Will you be all right?" Tom yelled across the driveway.

"Yeah, I'll be fine. Thanks for the lift. Bye Addie."

I woke up at the sound of my name and grinned. "Bye Jeanine."

She skipped across the walkway and headed inside. I stared at the mansion and wondered what it must be like to live there now that her brother was gone. My mind flashed back to a time when Ricky had stuck his head through my car window. When I was rescuing Jeanine after he had thrown a weekend party and trashed the place.

"Maybe we should stop by tomorrow," Tom suggested. "Her parents are going out of town. It's not safe for her to stay in that big house by herself."

"Sound familiar?" I saw Jeanine through her bedroom window and smiled.

She waved at us and then moved away from the window. I gave the mansion one last look as Tom pulled the car away. Something about it felt ominous.

Tom kept his eyes on the road while I studied his every move. Jeanine was his cousin, but I couldn't be sure if they ever really acknowledged it or not. They *were* related. But no one had raised them that way. Then again, maybe to care about someone, that wasn't necessary.

"Do you think she's okay?" I asked. "She never talks about him."

"It's summer. Maybe the two of you should have a sleepover."

"Hey!" I slapped his shoulder with a giggle, and Tom laughed.

"I think she's doing the best she can," he said. "I mean, we're all trying to raise ourselves here."

Good point.

"Was I too quiet in the car? I hope she doesn't think I was blowing her off."

Tom gripped the steering wheel and pulled out of the gated community. "I'm sure she noticed that you were acting weird. But she said that the minute we showed up today."

"Yeah, you're right."

I looked out the window and thought about the past twenty-four hours.

Nicki's bloody wrists and that bloody note.

It felt like something was happening here. Savannah was deadly.

"So are you gonna tell me what's going on?" He picked up speed once we were on the main road. "When you came to class today, why were you acting so weird?"

I bit my lip and struggled on the inside. Lately, I was always so distracted.

"Is it about Nicki? Did you talk to her?"

I spaced out, losing my train of thought. Apparently, it was easy to do today.

"Come on, Addie. What did she say?" he said, applying the pressure.

"I think Nicki's cutting herself."

He blinked, leaving one hand on the wheel. "You mean..."

"A straight razor and her wrist." I watched him, hoping he got the point.

"Damn." He furrowed his brow, looking out at the horizon.

"I know." It felt good to tell someone. But how to get her help?

"I know you and Nicki haven't been the best of friends."

"Yeah, but I don't want to see her hurting herself!" I didn't mean to raise my voice. But somehow, with everything that had happened with Ricky, I felt partially responsible.

"Look, let's just think about this. Your mom's a doctor. Couldn't she help?"

I hadn't thought of that.

"That's actually a really good idea." I tapped my finger against the car door. "I'll try to talk to her tonight. She might have already seen something like this."

"You think Caldwell knows?"

Nicki was the light of his life—an only child he loved to spoil rotten.

"There's something else." I folded my fingers

together.

"Okay," he accepted. "What?"

"Has anyone ever told you what happened to Nicki's mother?"

"No."

I looked at him. "She killed herself."

"What? When?" He stopped at a red light looking shocked.

"Not long after Nicki was born."

"Why didn't I know about this?"

"You haven't been at Maple Creek High that long. And no one really talks about it."

"Wow." Tom turned into a bobble head, looking from the road to me.

When we reached my house, Tom parked and took my hand. I searched his golden eyes and touched his face, prickled with stubble. He leaned into me, and I teased him before our lips finally met.

The past twelve hours had been too much. I wanted to forget it all and get lost in him.

His hand settled along my back as I crawled into his lap, craving his touch. Tom gave me the softest kiss and I sighed, happy that this part of my life had been left alone. My back slammed into the steering wheel, and the horn went off while I sat on top of him.

Laughter filled the air, because I was the least likely person to be caught making out in a car. But we were in the wilderness, and my parents weren't home. Somehow, blush stained my cheeks anyway. Tom used his thumb like a paint brush, pretending to wipe it away.

When he looked at me, I leaned my forehead against his. Tom held me in his arms and I closed my eyes, wondering if my life would ever be considered normal. Deep down, I knew that the only stability I really needed was him.

"There's something I need to tell you."

My daydream interrupted, I opened my eyes and glanced up at him.

"I think we should go into the woods tonight."

## Chapter 4

**H**ow long will you be gone?" I saw the bags by the door and tried not to look so disappointed. I shouldn't have been surprised. This was Jeffrey and Eleanor we were talking about. They were never reliable or responsible or *here.*

"A few days," Eleanor chimed, yelling to Jeffrey in the kitchen.

"It's really nice that you still make time for each other." I caught her eye, hoping she knew what I had implied. They penciled romance into the schedule, but never me.

Eleanor smiled—a plastic one that could have passed for artificial corn syrup. As if the real stuff wasn't artificial enough.

"Come on, honey! We're going to be late." She checked herself in the mirror and fastened her dark hair back with a barrette. Her clothing was anything but casual—formal evening wear with heels. She even had her pearls on.

But like I said—I shouldn't have been surprised.

Eleanor Jacobs hadn't relaxed a day in her life.

"Mom, before you go." I blocked her passage to the foyer. "I wanted to talk to you about something."

Eleanor set her purse down on the end table and sighed. "Okay."

"Well, something happened at school today." I pressed my thumb into my palm, praying for the right words to come. "Nothing actually happened. Well, it had already happened, I guess."

"Spit it out, Addie." She applied a dab of lipstick. "I don't have all day."

"Okay." I stood up straight and started to sweat. What was wrong with me?

Why was it so hard for me to have a conversation with the woman I had once believed to be my mother? I guess she still was, though not literally. Not biologically.

Just on paper.

"Tom and I were talking about it in the car today. You know, on the way back from school?" It sounded like I was asking her a question. *Was I asking her a question?*

"Oh." One word from Eleanor, and I went pale. "I think I know what this is about."

"You do?" I cocked my head to the side, finding that very hard to believe.

"Yes." She pointed down with a smile. "You stay right here. I've got just the thing."

Confused, I lingered in the foyer and sighed. Since when could she read minds?

"Hey, kiddo!" Jeffrey approached with his luggage and a briefcase. "Looks like we're off." He glanced down at the other bags and asked, "Where did your mother go?"

"I don't know, but she'll be right back."

"You'll be fine here by yourself, right?" He grinned like a two-year-old.

"Have you *ever* considered whether or not I would be fine here by myself?"

"What?" He acted like I had just spoken in a foreign language.

"Never mind," I said. My words were laced with acid. "I just find it strange that you've always had time to run off to a medical convention with Mom. Even though you're an attorney."

"Addie, your mother and I make time for each other. We're married," he muttered.

"Yeah." I shut my eyes as a migraine kicked in. "I know."

"Speak of the devil and she will appear." Jeffrey winked as Eleanor returned.

"Why don't you load the car?" she encouraged, pointing at all the luggage.

"Oh, yeah." He opened the door and tried to carry everything out at once. I heard objects breaking as he dropped a bag on the porch. "Bye, Addie. Have fun!"

Eleanor shut the door and tried to keep her cool. I'm sure most of the stuff he was breaking was hers.

She smiled and handed me a small bag. "It's called a prophylactic."

I unzipped the bag, and there must have been fifty condoms inside.

My mouth dropped wide open as I turned red as a cherry. "Mom."

"Addie, there's nothing to be nervous about. Intimacy is a gift from God. You should be perfectly comfortable with your sexuality. I want you and Tom to be healthy and safe."

"Oh. My. God." I wanted to crawl under a rock and hide.

"I'm glad you don't have to stay here alone. But I wasn't born yesterday."

"What is that supposed to mean?" I scoffed.

Horrified, I shoved the bag of condoms into her chest and stormed off. There must have been every color of latex and rubber imaginable. And flavor, too, I guess.

"It means I know he spends the night with you. I just want you to be prepared."

With a deep exhale, I spun around and bit my lip. "How do you know what Tom and I do when you're not here? Even if he does stay over, at least he's keeping me safe."

"And that's wonderful, but I want you to be safe when it comes to sex, too."

I shoved my fingers in my hair and groaned.

"So what? You think we're irresponsible?"

"I didn't say that. But you're teenagers, Addie." Her hand was on her hip.

"So you think Tom and I would just... without..."

"Addie, what you do with your boyfriend is not what concerns me. It's *how* you do it."

"We're not even doing anything!" I went pale after the words left my lips.

Eleanor brought her brows together and pursed her lips. "Okay."

It wasn't until she walked out the door that I realized she didn't believe me.

She left the condoms on the table by the door.

Jeffrey backed the car out of the garage, and they disappeared into the wilderness. I waited a few more minutes and screamed, scattering the condoms on the floor. She was probably talking about me now, telling her husband that I had lied about having sex with Tom.

She hadn't even given me the chance to ask about Nicki.

That infuriated me the most. I could have used her help. But now I was on my own.

I stomped my way up the staircase and wondered if I should have been having sex with Tom. Clearly, I had the Eleanor Jacobs stamp of approval. I guess she thought we were twisting the sheets every time they walked out the door.

Shaking it off, I waltzed into my bedroom and soared onto the mattress.

My first weekend of summer break, and my parents were already gone.

Some things never change.

\* \* \*

My spirits lifted when the doorbell rang. Jeffrey and Eleanor had left hours ago, and it was already dark outside. I hadn't eaten dinner yet, so I was starving.

To be honest, I had been sulking in my room for the better part of the afternoon.

I spotted Tom through the window, and he waved. That warm, buzzy feeling swam through me. Not because we were going to be alone together. I always felt like that whenever he came around. Maybe it was the excitement of having him near.

I stepped into the foyer, and my heart dropped.

Condoms lay scattered across the floor. I put my hand over my mouth as Tom knocked on the door. How could I forget to get rid of these? Especially after my outrage?

"Just a second!" I scrambled to grab them all, depositing them back into the bag.

Tom must have thought I was incompetent if it took me this long to open the door.

"It's unlocked!" he yelled from the porch. "Can I just come in?"

My face turned seven shades of red as I saw the door knob twist. I slipped the last couple into the bag and jumped to my feet when he opened the door. Forcing a smile, I kept my hands behind my back to conceal the bag from his sight. Until I could hide it.

"Hey." He gave me a handsome smile and came closer, leaning in.

"Hey," I echoed, turning my cheek when he leaned in for a kiss.

That was probably meant for my lips, but I couldn't even give him a hug right now.

"Are you okay?" Tom reached out to grab my hands, then noticed that they were behind my back. His eyes lingered there, and he stepped to the side to investigate.

"Yeah, yeah," I stuttered. I had never been a very good liar. "I'm fine."

"Okay." He chuckled. But I couldn't tell if he was perplexed or amused.

"Just give me a minute to take care of something." I held his gaze and walked backwards, planning to toss these in the trash before he noticed.

"Wait." He touched my shoulders and backed me into the wall.

"What?" I was impatient, but for good reason.

I was carrying enough condoms to line the Panama Canal.

Tom kissed me, and my eyes slid closed. Every bit of worry drifted away. I felt my body relaxing at his touch. It was releasing whatever had left me wound too tight.

As I went to curl my arms around his neck, I forgot the bag.

It hit the floor, and condoms spewed everywhere.

Tom pulled back, and I was scared to look.

"Addie, is there something you need to tell me?"

I burrowed my head in his chest, searching for a hole to crawl into.

"Addie." He bent over and I grabbed his arm, trying to hold him back. But he was too strong. Before I knew it, Tom was squatting down and sifting through all the colors.

"Look, it's not what you think." I felt flushed and heated. I wanted to hide.

He took a knee and looked up at me, waiting for an explanation.

"I was trying to tell Mom about Nicki. But she jumped to conclusions and thought I was talking about us. The next thing I knew, she was giving me the safe sex talk."

Tom rubbed his jaw and studied the condoms. Then he stood up with a sigh.

I caught his eye, and he pulled me into his arms. It was a sweet hug meant to comfort me. I sank into his embrace and loved the feel of his arms around me.

"She used the word prophylactic and everything. It was horrible."

Tom lifted my chin and cupped my cheek in his hand. "I'm sorry."

Pulling out of his embrace, I bent down and slid all of the condoms into the bag in one swoop. Then I marched into the kitchen and opened the trash can.

"Wait." Tom appeared behind me. "Maybe you shouldn't get rid of *all* of them."

"What?" I wondered if this could get any more awkward.

"Well, I mean, after last night. Don't you want to be careful? Just in case—"

I dropped the bag on the counter and brushed past him, ready to rip my hair out.

"Addie, you've been giving me a lot of mixed signals lately."

I stopped and turned around to face him. He had followed me into the living room.

"What? You thought tonight we were going to..." I felt my pulse thrum.

Tom reached into his pocket and pulled out a condom. Blood drained from my face, and I forgot how to breathe. He had come prepared, bringing protection of his own.

What was worse—there were two of them.

I walked out the door and darted into the woods.

"Addie!" I heard Tom calling my name. I knew he would come after me.

But the dark, lofty forest looked like a mirage. Some false dream designed to entice and entrap me. I had never felt so easily swayed, so willing to flee, so eager to run.

"Addie!"

I zigged and zagged through the forest, holding on to a tree to catch my breath. When I thought about it, he had every right to be confused. Last night, I had practically climbed on top of him and screamed, *Take me now.* But I didn't feel that way tonight.

"Are you going to tell me what's going on in that head of yours?"

I looked back at Tom and then stared at the ground. "I'm sorry."

"Last night, I was the one holding back. And now you're saying the exact opposite of what you said then." He gestured towards me, fighting to catch his breath.

He was right. I was on the fence. I couldn't make up my mind.

"Which is it, Addie? I'm crazy about you, but I can only take so much!"

"I'm not ready!" I screamed, glad no one could hear us.

Tom put his hands on his hips and huffed. "What?"

"Yes, last night I was—in that moment. But if I really think about it..."

"You're not ready." His voice was soft, smooth. He was listening to me.

I shook my head, a little terrified of how he was going to react.

"Addie." He leaned against the tree I was clinging to. "I'm not the one who brought this up in the first place. If you think I'm going to pressure you, you're wrong."

"I never thought that. It's just—"

"Because I'm the guy?" he filled in.

"Well." I thought about it for a second. "Yeah."

"Addie." He took a step closer. "I've waited for you for almost ten years. *Trust me*, I've got more patience than the average male."

I laughed, scraping my teeth against my lip. "Sorry. I guess I forget that sometimes."

"Come here." He rested his hand at the small of my back as I leaned into him.

"I know it's stupid, me acting like this. But I've just had a really weird day."

"I love you," he whispered. "And I'm not going anywhere."

His hand cradled my neck, and it felt like heaven. "I love you, too."

With a sigh of frustration, Tom scanned the forest and bit his lip. "Let's go inside." He stroked my arm and pulled me in close. "Have you had anything to eat?"

I shook my head and looked down. "No."

"C'mon." He led me towards the house. "Let's forget about all this."

Relief swept through me as we headed back. I wrapped my arms around him, and he planted a kiss on my head. Walking hand and hand, I suddenly felt less afraid.

Of the future. Of sex. Of that bloody message

and whatever it meant.

I had a boyfriend who was wise beyond his years. He may have been trapped in the body of a teenager. But Tom was more mature than some men in their twenties.

I knew that this didn't happen very often—I was just lucky.

Back at the house, I sat down on the kitchen counter and watched him work. Since we met, I kept the pantry and fridge stocked with food for when he came over and cooked. Before Tom, I had relied on things like Lucky Charms and Chef Boyardee.

With him, it felt like I had a world-renowned chef on hand. He loved to cook, but rarely had the opportunity to in that empty mansion. I knew he must have learned all of his tips and tricks from Daniel. By using the same recipes, Tom was keeping his memory alive.

"Want a taste?" Tom pointed at a pot of tomato sauce.

I swung my legs off the edge with a beaming nod.

Enjoying my zeal, Tom grabbed a wooden spoon and dipped it into the sauce. Then he came closer and held a hand out beneath the spoon in case he spilled any. I opened my mouth and nibbled at the outer rim, not wanting to burn my tongue.

"Do you like it?" he wondered, searching my eyes.

"Yeah, it's ready." I took the spoon so I could lick the rest off. "You've got it just right."

Tom grinned, happy to hear my praise. Once the wooden spoon was clean, I rinsed it off in the sink and watched him serve our plates. He sprinkled chunks of mozzarella over the pasta and then set aside bread and a garden salad.

"You spoil me." I put my head on his back and curled my arms around his chest.

Tom turned around until our torsos were flush. I felt his breath on my face and shut my eyes, running my fingers over his shoulders and down his shirtsleeves.

"I don't know what I'd do if I didn't have you," I whispered.

Tom cupped my cheek in his hand and tilted my face towards his.

"You'd be just fine," he muttered. "Just like you were before you met me."

I furrowed my brow, struggling to decipher his meaning.

"You're stronger than you think you are," he explained. "But I'm glad I have you, too."

I leaned up on my tippy toes to kiss him, and then stared into his eyes.

"What?" he chuckled, pushing my hair over my shoulders.

"You don't own me, you know." I batted my lashes, playing, teasing, flirting.

"Is that right?" he cocked his brow. "Well then, I guess that means you don't own me either."

He smirked and carried our plates to the table, where I took a seat and smiled.

For the first few minutes, neither of us said a word. I was too busy twirling noodles around my fork and swallowing as fast as possible. Even Tom was exceptionally hungry. But considering the fact that it was after eight o' clock on a Friday night, I could see why.

"So why do you want to go into the woods tonight?" I asked.

Tom took a breath and wiped his mouth. "You know why."

His golden eyes centered on me, and I looked away.

"But come on, Tom. This can't actually be—"

"Like last time?" He stabbed his salad with a fork, and I heard the metal scrap the bowl. When he looked at me again, a shudder traveled down my spine.

"But—"

"Addison," he scolded.

Fire shot through my veins, as I glared straight ahead.

My own father had never called me by my first name before. Whoever he was.

Feeling belittled, I pushed my chair back and stormed out of the room. What gave him the right to act so high and mighty? Just because he thought he knew it all.

"Addie." Tom followed me into the living room and grabbed my arm.

"No," I snapped, spinning around. "I don't want to go into the woods tonight."

"Why not?" he challenged. "You already have. Technically."

His sarcasm couldn't have come at a worse time.

"You know what I mean."

Tom stroked the stubble on his cheeks and muttered something under his breath.

"It's over. All of it." I sank down on the couch. "I don't want to do this again."

"Are you living in some kind of dream world?" Tom leaned over me and shook my arms. "Wake up, Addie! It's happening again whether you like it or not."

Last spring had been hell. It had taken me a very long time to get to where I was now. And that wasn't saying a whole lot. I was still a nervous wreck, and it had only been a month.

Tom sat down beside me and took my hand, circling his thumb over my wrist.

"It's just to check," he soothed. "So we'll have options."

I gave him a faint nod. "Okay," I surrendered. "Let's do it now."

Tom got off the couch and went into the garage. I heard him rifling around out there but failed to move an inch. The thing is—I was still in denial. In fact, I was so far gone that I couldn't see the forest for the trees. Tom saw everything. And he was always right.

When I looked up, Tom was waiting for me in the foyer. So I dragged myself to the front door and locked it behind us. Then I crossed my fingers and said a quick prayer.

We headed into the woods with two flashlights and a shovel.

# Chapter 5

Two Weeks Earlier...

It was dark at first. All shadows. No light.

Cob webs hung from the ceiling as I stepped into the darkness. There was a staircase. One that led to the third story. A place I'd never been before.

The door shut and I gasped. "Tom!"

"Sorry." He put his hand around my waist. "I thought it would stay open."

Sighing, I climbed the staircase with my hand on the rail. Tom stayed behind, ready to catch me should I fall. The wooden steps creaked beneath my feet, startling me at first.

"Have you ever been up here before?" I asked.

"No." His breath touched the back of my neck. "The door was always locked, so I never thought anything of it."

I reached the top of the steps and turned

around. "You were never curious?"

Tom looked up at me. "I asked Grandpa one time. He said it was just a bunch of junk in the attic."

Light poured in through a window near the ceiling. It was the first thing I saw.

With a shallow breath, I took his hand and stepped into the room.

"What is this place?" Tom said.

My eyes searched the attic as I let go of his hand. At the center of the room lay an island of glass cases. Like the ones you see at a jewelry store.

"It looks like a museum." Tom went on ahead of me, looking around.

Paintings hung on every wall. But they weren't Daniel's work. Not all of them.

Rembrandt. Monet. Van Gogh.

The artwork alone was worth millions.

"Where did he get all these?" My head was spinning. I remembered something Eleanor told me—Daniel was heir to a family fortune. Now I knew how he had spent some of it.

"I don't know." Tom crossed his arms and circled the room.

"These are worth millions." I pointed at the paintings, and his brow shot up. "Why would he keep them here? I mean, this isn't exactly the safest place."

Tom shrugged. "Maybe it is."

His golden eyes flickered beneath the light.

"How?" I took a step towards him—a moth to the flame.

"Out here in the woods, in the middle of nowhere." He shoved his hands in his pockets and thrummed his fingers over a display case. "It's the last place anyone would look."

I wrapped my arms around him and put my head on his back. With Daniel gone, Tom was the only soft place to land. He took my hands and turned around, tilting my chin up.

"Do you think things will ever be the same again?" I asked.

He touched my cheek and looked down. "No."

His hand dropped from my skin and he walked away.

"Do you mean between us?" I felt like crying.

"Addie, I don't know what you want me to say."

I pulled at his shoulder until he turned around. But he looked away.

"I want you to be honest with me."

He nodded. "Okay."

"So what is it?" Tears burned the back of my eyes. "You don't want me anymore?"

"No, I never said that. But maybe we just need some space."

"Space?" My mouth went dry. "You want space?"

"Addie, you live next door."

I furrowed my brow. "What's that supposed to

mean?"

"It's just that I need time to figure this out. Get my head straight, whatever."

I nodded and took a step away from him. "Fine," I murmured. There were tears in my eyes. "You can have all the space you want."

"Addie."

I ran down the staircase and dried my eyes.

I had to get out of here. I had to get out of this house.

Ever since the funeral, I had been clinging to the hope of recovering in Tom's arms. I thought he would heal me, like I wanted to heal him. But he wouldn't let me. He didn't want me. Without Daniel in this big house, I felt unwelcome and alone.

The door jammed at the bottom of the stairs. I twisted the handle and kicked the door, desperate to get out of here. Especially when Tom barreled down the steps behind me.

"What is it?" he said.

"This damn door won't open!" I turned my back to him and kicked it one last time.

"That's not going to help." He grabbed the doorknob and pushed against the frame.

"Well, why don't you figure it out then?"

I crossed my arms and sat down on the bottom step with a huff. Of course we would be locked in a room together when I couldn't stand the sight of him. The more he pushed me away, the more I realized how badly I not only *needed* but *wanted* him.

"I think you messed up the lock," he assessed. "What did you do?"

"Nothing!" I whined. "I was just trying to get out of here! Away from you!"

He froze and then turned around, looking at me.

"Doesn't feel so good, does it?" I grumbled. "When the shoe is on the other foot?"

He came over and sat down beside me. I tucked my elbows in so we wouldn't touch.

"It has nothing to do with you," he said. "It's me. All me."

"I don't want to be with someone that I love more than they love me."

"Well, you're not," he hissed. "Who said anything about not loving you?"

"Ever since Daniel died, I have felt like I was drowning!" I cried, catching him off guard. "I've *wanted* you and *needed* you. Since when did you stop needing me?"

I went to stand and Tom grabbed my arm. Then his hand slipped around my waist and he pulled me into his lap. Even though I wanted to resist, he cast those amber eyes upon me— scorching like honey in fire. And I was a goner.

When his lips touched mine, I ran my fingers through his hair and let myself fall. He cradled my body in his arms and kissed me again. More passionately this time.

It was like kissing someone new. The way he

evolved in that moment.

His fingertips glided beneath my shirt as I leaned my head back. Then his mouth was on my neck, and I shut my eyes with a sigh. He kissed his way across my collarbone and then pushed my shirtsleeve down my arm. Everything prickled with delight.

"I do love you," he whispered. "More than you know."

Leaning closer, I brushed my mouth against his and grappled with his shirt.

"Not here," he said. "Not now."

I pressed my forehead to his and kept my arms around him.

"I want it to be special." He cupped my cheek. "I want it to be right."

"Yeah," I agreed, biting my lip. "And it will be."

We kissed—a series of quick pecks. And then the door creaked open.

I looked back in Tom's arms, wondering if I should be afraid.

"Sometimes, I think this place might be haunted," I said.

"Sometimes, I'm not so sure it isn't."

He set me down and we never talked about the secret room again.

But I thought about it all the time. Especially those first few weeks back at school. When the town was swarming with gossip about what really happened that night.

That was when the dreams started. Not the nightmares. Those were already in full bloom by then. And there were plenty more to come.

But the dreams were the first real time my psyche had a rest.

They came to me at night. Sweet dreams. Quite a juxtaposition to the terrors awaiting me every time my head hit the pillow. They were like tonic water—a sudden relief.

I could never remember what they were about. But they were strong enough to rouse me from sleep. Not in the way the nightmares had. It felt more like Sleeping Beauty. And when I had one of those sweet dreams, they always kissed me awake.

One night I woke up and ran to Tom's house like a puppet on a string.

He was wide awake, up listening to music, all alone in the mansion.

"Hey." He rose with a furrowed brow. "It's the middle of the night."

"I know," I panted, "but I have to see something."

Sweat ran down my back as I climbed the staircase. I made it up one flight and then two, before Tom finally caught up with me. He grabbed my arm to pull me back. But it was like someone had magnetized me to this place.

"I have to go upstairs," I said. "I need to check something."

"Let me go with you."

I darted into the room with Antoinette's portrait, but it was gone.

"Where is the painting?" I looked back at Tom.

"I don't know." He scratched his head, perplexed. "It was here the last time I checked."

It was worse than I expected. The dreams hadn't prepared me for this.

I opened the door and went up to the attic. What else had been taken?

"Do you think we should call the cops?" Tom yelled up the staircase.

I ignored him and turned the corner. Then I circled the island, shifting from display case to display case. I ran my fingers over the glass and then stopped in my tracks.

Tom came into the attic. "If someone was here, then—"

I stared for the longest time. It couldn't be that easy. Could it?

I slid across the glass and landed on the other side. Then I opened the back of the display case with the same key I had used to get in the attic. Clever thinking—fashioning a key for the two of us that would open all the doors, unlock all of Daniel's secrets.

"Addie, what is going on?" Tom breathed down my neck.

I looked into the palm of my hand and turned around.

"I found it."

His eyes widened in shock. I recognized the look. He almost didn't believe me.

I set it down on the counter and let it stare up at us.

The elusive emerald necklace.

"What do we do now?" I asked.

Tom picked up the necklace in his hand. "Bury it."

## Chapter 6

With every step I took into the forest, my heart beat faster. The sun had set, but the air was far from cool and light. I tried to keep that in mind as I walked through the grass.

Typically, I was pretty cooperative. But I saw no need in digging up the past. As if that bloody note weren't enough. Now he wanted more proof that my life was a living hell.

"Is this it?" I don't know why I asked. I already knew.

"Yeah." Tom surveyed the live oak before us— all soaring height and sturdy limbs. The kind of tree you wouldn't want nestled too closely to a car or house. Because it had the capacity to do more than damage. A tower like that was meant to destroy.

My skin prickled with fear as I looked over my shoulder. We were deep in the woods, at least a mile from my house. Something about the distance shot a shiver down my spine.

"Hold this." Tom handed me his flashlight and then took a step back with the shovel. Veins were springing to life all over his arms, as he pierced the ground on a quest for dirt.

Mosquitos were in the air, so I swatted them away and sat down in the grass. Even with the sun put to bed, it was still hot and humid in the air. All the while, Tom kept at it, piling dirt off to the side as he dug deeper and deeper.

Tom took a break and relaxed, leaning on the shovel. Sweat brimmed over his brow, while he used the tail of his shirt to wipe it off. When he started up again, I watched his body move beneath the moonlight, wondering what it would be like to move with him.

"I wish we'd brought some water," he panted.

"Do you want me to get you some?" I offered.

"Nah." He shook his head and spit in the dirt. "If you walk to your house and back, that could take almost an hour." He swatted at a mosquito. "I'm almost done anyway."

Time dragged on as he excavated the ground.

It was rich, brown Savannah soil.

The kind nourished by a nearby stream.

Desperate for a peek, I approached the hole he had carved out of the earth. As I stared at the empty space, some sort of dread coursed through me. Perhaps I was astounded at how vulnerable even a patch of land was—so easily pillaged at the hand of man.

Eventually Tom took his shirt off and threw the shovel down. Sweat ran in rivulets down his chiseled body, and I couldn't take my eyes off those abs. With a torso like that, Tom could have been on the cover of a magazine. My mouth went dry and I swallowed, amazed that he was only seventeen. Based on looks alone, he could pass for twenty-three.

"Addie," he called. And from the sound of it, that hadn't been the first time he had said my name.

I wiped the drool from my mouth and said, "Yeah."

"I'm so thirsty." He ran his fingers through his hair. "I need water."

"Why don't you let me get you some?" I peered up at Tom and touched his leg.

He looked into my eyes, trying to read my mind. "Addie, I don't know if that's safe."

Tom wiped his brow and picked up the shovel. When he resumed his work, I stood up and brushed the dust off my shorts. He was perspiring enough to be in the Mojave Desert. And when I saw how much he had left to dig, my throat clenched with guilt.

"There's a creek not too far from here." I looked over his shoulder in that direction. But his eyes stayed on me. "I can bring you some back."

"I don't know. Maybe I should go with you."

"No, I'll be fine. Just keep digging."

He appraised the determined look on my face with a sigh.

"Unless you want to have a heat stroke in the middle of the night."

"All right," he said.

"I won't be long," I promised, already on my way.

"Be careful." His voice followed me in the night as he resumed digging.

I left Tom with a flashlight and used the other to find my way to the creek. As a child, I had wandered down this path too often. Plunging into the wilderness to escape a life I had rather leave behind. Even then, I knew my parents were too worse for wear.

It's not normal to force children to fend for themselves. Was it selfishness? Materialism? Eleanor's constant need to keep up with the Joneses?

Or was it all because I was adopted?

Because I wasn't really theirs?

Because, sometimes, I wondered whether they ever actually wanted me at all.

I turned my flashlight off as the moon came into view. Tom must have been a few acres away by now, because I couldn't see him anymore. I knew these woods well, but maybe I had overestimated my abilities in the dark. Most of my excursions had taken place when the sun was up. With the exception of times when I hadn't cared if I didn't make it out of the wilderness alive.

A hoot owl made me flinch, as I shined my light over the nocturnal creature. Breathing a sigh of relief, I kept on my journey with a quicker stride. My heart was beating so fast.

Every time I felt a thorn scratch or heard a twig snap, I held my breath. But I kept moving. Desperate to escape the shadows of the forest—a place I had once called home.

The woods meant something different now. And I couldn't be sure which moment had redefined them. Sexual Assault? Violence? Murder?

Every time I touched down on Savannah soil it made me tremble. When Tom was with me, it made things easier. I felt less afraid.

But what about now—when he was not?

I heard running water up ahead and ran the rest of the way to the creek. I was shaking by the time I reached the river bank and knelt down to dip my hands in the water. It was cool despite the summer heat, so I lapped up what I could.

Next came the hurdle of figuring out a way to transport the water back to Tom. It wasn't like I could carry liquid in my pockets. I searched for an object—a plastic cup or something made of glass. A beer bottle maybe.

This deep into the woods, hunters trespassed during deer season. With all this virgin land, I was sure of it. And while their litter might not be the most sanitary option, it was the only one we had. That is—if I could find any.

Using a flashlight, I followed the stream and spotted a soda can. Orange Crush. It was a frothy concoction of sugary goodness. More syrup than fruit. But all that remained was an empty can powdered with mud.

I crouched down and stared at the used can, knowing I could never serve fresh water in that. Not to Tom. The last thing I wanted was for him to dodge a heat stroke and then get tetanus.

Footsteps.

They sent fear through my veins like a shot of cocaine. I hid behind the embankment and waited, that orange soda can the last thing on my mind.

Hushed whispers rattled in my eardrums. I tried to make out the voices.

One of them whistled and then they left. My heart was beating so loud that I couldn't even breathe. I was frozen to that spot, my butt on the bank.

But then something popped in the distance.

It sounded like a gunshot, but not quite. Speechless, I stayed down and waited. With every second that passed, my heart skipped a beat. I couldn't breathe, didn't want to.

Because it just might kill me.

I bit into my lower lip and swayed enough to hide behind a tree.

If strangers were near, what about Tom? He was deep in the woods digging a hole.

A hole we couldn't let anyone else see. Maybe

because of what lay at the bottom.

Frantic with fear, I leapt up in an attempt to run. But then there were voices again.

A first. A second. A *third*.

Ducking behind another tree, I scanned the forest until I spotted them. Three emerging figures in the distance. And they were carrying flashlights, too.

I walked backwards until I was out of their line of sight and then bolted the rest of the way to Tom. When I arrived, beads of sweat were rippling down his body. But I didn't have time for my raging female hormones to be jumping up and down right now.

"Stop!" I hissed, coming to a halt like a baseball player slides into home base.

"What are you doing?" He grabbed my wrist and helped me up.

"Someone's coming."

If there had been a moment of hesitation, I might not be telling you this story right now.

But Tom didn't question me. Instead, he hurried to fill the hole with dirt, while I shoved as much as I could in with my bare hands.

When flashlights flickered in the distance, Tom cursed under his breath. The hole might resemble a flat patch, if the viewer were in complete and total darkness. But our visitors were aided by a flashlight, so Tom pushed at my back until I was behind the tree.

"Give me your foot," he whispered.

I hiked my leg up in the air as he gave me a boost, then scaled my way to the top. Tom climbed up after me and wrapped his arm around my waist. Voices came closer, but we were cleverly hidden behind the lofty branches, and high enough to have the advantage.

I looked back at him, as he hovered over me. With his bare skin everywhere, I felt so protected and warm. Tom was no teenage boy. He was a grown man.

He already stood over six feet and had the makings of a full-grown beard.

I looked up at him and ran my hand over his back, wishing things were different. Tom lowered his head and curled my body into his, shielding me where the tree couldn't. Before I knew it, they were upon us.

We heard footsteps down below. Then a piercing cry echoed across the wilderness.

I swayed back and Tom kept me steady, clasping his hand over my mouth.

The flickering lights went out, and the strangers down below disappeared.

After counting to a hundred, Tom jumped down and filled the rest of the hole with dirt. Thunder and lightning erupted in the sky overhead, as I climbed out of the tree. Tom left the shovel on the ground and we made a run for it, sprinting to the house as fast as we could.

By the time we made it there, it was too late.

The door was standing wide open, and there

were obvious signs of forced entry.

The TV was on in the living room, even though it was off when we left. A news reporter was talking about two men on trial for murder, who had recently escaped from prison.

The first—someone I knew very well as a beautiful criminal with piercing blue eyes.

The second—my worst nightmare in human form, Tony DeMilo.

The biggest mystery of all was not *how* they escaped, but with *who?*

CTV footage showed a third figure that had let them out. But the image was obscured.

Now I knew who had been lurking in the woods for the past couple of nights.

DeMilo was back. And I knew what he wanted.

That note was written in blood for a reason.

*Find the necklace.*

Because if I didn't, he just might kill me.

# Chapter 7

I felt breathless, lying awake in bed. Lightning flashed in the evening sky, and I wondered if it would always be like this. Would Tom always be here?

Would I always feel so... *afraid?*

The covers felt like a noose around my neck, so I kicked them aside and inhaled. I heard the shower in the bathroom and a thrill raced through me.

I stared at the ceiling, opening and closing my eyes, imagining a future with Tom. He was everything I had ever wanted and more. But what if the time to have him was now?

With DeMilo on the run, every moment was as fragile as the last. Because it might very well be our last. We were just seventeen. But how much time did we really have?

Listening to the running water, I slipped out of

bed and walked towards the door. It was a magnetic force that pulled me there, pulling me to him. Almost like I couldn't help it.

I put my ear to the door and ran my fingers down my arm. Goosebumps popped up on my skin like the blood racing through my veins. I bit my lip to hold myself back, but I didn't have a will of iron. I wasn't like Tom. For me, there was no restraint left.

I was his. Completely. What happened next was up to him.

I twisted the doorknob and blushed once I realized it was unlocked. Lately, he had been a master at putting up walls. But Tom hadn't kept me out. Not tonight. He'd left the door unlocked— a chance for me to come in if I wished.

Feeling brazen, I opened the door and slipped inside. He was the one who spent years watching me in the forest. But now I was the voyeur, stalking and looming too close.

I could make out his silhouette behind the frosted glass. As he ran his fingers through his hair, I wondered if it would be so wrong—to open the shower door and ask him.

Ask him to love me.

The water shut off and I froze, sapped of my will power. Tom slid the door back and grabbed a towel, while I lowered my eyes and looked away. Blush seared across my cheeks like a branding iron. Steam billowed like clouds overhead, and I couldn't breathe.

Tom stepped out with the towel around his waist, startled to find me there.

He pierced me with a golden gaze, his irises like scorching ocher. Or honey. Or caramel. Or whiskey. There was sweetness to the color, paired with something bitter.

"What are you doing in here?" He smoothed his wet locks back with the touch of his hand. In this lighting, his hair was so black it almost looked blue. Like Elvis.

"I umm..." I fluttered my lashes, unable to describe the way he made me feel.

Tom narrowed his eyes, and I couldn't stand the heat.

"Umm." I grabbed the handle on the door behind me. But not with the intention to flee. I needed something stable, something to lean on. Because I was weak in the knees.

I closed my eyes and ran my fingers through my hair, struggling for air. It was stifling in here. But I knew that had nothing to do with the steam.

When I looked up, Tom was standing right in front of me. Everything about him looked like a man. His height, his strength—not to mention his pecs and arms and abs.

Droplets of water rippled down his skin, and my tongue went dry in my mouth.

"Why did you come in here?" His breath was on my face, warm and nice.

I searched his eyes and reached out. Before I could touch him, Tom took my hand and put it on his chest. Right over his beating heart.

"I've just been feeling really scared," I confessed. "I know we're young. But we may not have much time left. What if tonight is all we have?"

He lowered his eyes and put a finger to my lips. "Shh..."

I felt weightless, slowly turning into a puddle of goo. It was a spell he had cast. I was charmed, fixated, so in love with the boy from my dream. Only it wasn't a dream.

He brushed his thumb against my lips, and I felt sparks. His touch was electric.

"Do you remember that lecture we had in English class?"

He cupped my cheek with a silent laugh. "Leave it to you to bring up school at a time like this." His eyes were liquid amber, and he had sealed my soul inside of them.

"About the Roman poet," I murmured. "*Carpe diem*. It means to—"

"Seize the day." He tucked a lock of hair behind my ear and I shivered.

"Yeah." I swallowed and moistened my lips, sinking my teeth into the lower one.

"Well, the sun won't be up for hours."

When I chuckled, my cheek cuddled deeper into the palm of his hand.

"No, that's not what I mean." I touched his hand. "Do you know what I mean?"

He nodded with a heavy breath. "I think so."

"What if there is no tomorrow for us? What if all we have is today?"

"Addie." He shut his eyes and pinched the bridge of his nose. "I don't know if—"

"There are things I want to experience in life." I clung to the back of his neck. "Before I'm gone," I whimpered. "There are things I want to do. With you."

Tom flattened his hand on the door behind me. "Addie."

But my name on his lips was like a green light. And I just couldn't wait.

I kissed him as my nails sliced his back, a warning sign for the desperate love to come. Tom nipped at my lower lip and held me against the door, as we engaged in a tug-of-war for the ages. A push and pull of sorts—a force neither of us could resist.

Tom pulled back and I moaned, peering up at him like I had found salvation in his eyes. But he scanned my face and made an effort to steady himself, breathing gently.

I squirmed against the door, pulsing and pounding with desire. He bowed his head and kissed my shoulder, then took a breath and lifted it, touching his forehead to mine.

The question was stamped on his face—he didn't have to ask.

My fingers curled around his neck as I nodded with a breathy, "Yes."

When he rushed in to kiss me, I felt the smile

on his lips. Warmth spread through me like an untamed fire, and I tilted my head back to welcome his touch. Tom threaded his fingers in my hair and pulled me closer, grasping and clinging for what belonged to him.

As I wrapped my arms around him, Tom lifted me in the air. He held my face and gasped, crushing his lips to mine. I felt greedy and rushed, helpless without his touch.

My fingernails were clawing at his back as I held on tight, clinging to his body. Tom opened the door. And when he dropped me on the bed, I let out a strangled cry.

As he lowered his body to mine, I ran my hands over his back and sighed. For what felt like forever, this was what I had wanted. I didn't want to have sex with my boyfriend. No, I wanted the man of my dreams to make love to me.

"Maybe it's not so bad your mom gave you the sex talk," he joked.

"Shut up." I tugged him closer and he chuckled, trailing his fingers down my neck.

I sank into the mattress and made myself comfortable, staring up at the ceiling. Rain came in shadows across the walls, and I smiled. My first time was going to be right here—in my bedroom. And I couldn't think of a better spot. It was perfect.

"Ready?" Tom caged me in with his elbows as he hovered above me.

"Yeah." I feathered my fingers through his

hair. "I'm ready."

Tom shot me a crooked grin and touched the end of his nose to mine. "I love you," he whispered in the dark. Lightning flashed, illuminating his features. He was beautiful.

"I love you, too," I breathed, as my heart picked up speed.

A great big crash sounded downstairs, and it was like déjà vu all over again. Tom froze above me, staring into the open doorway. I dug my fingers into his back, cursing the fates.

Why couldn't the universe just let us have this moment together?

Before we were both dead.

"I have to go downstairs and see what that is," he whispered. "Stay here."

He climbed off the bed and got dressed, while I pulled the covers around me.

"Tom." I grabbed his hand. And when he looked at me, I saw it in his eyes.

Disappointment.

"We'll try again." He cradled my face and wrapped his arms around me.

You would think we were an older married couple trying to get pregnant. Not two teenagers who were having a hard time getting to home base.

Tom crept down the staircase as I slipped into his shirt.

Should we call the cops? Get a gun? Exchange my parents?

I didn't know what to do anymore. And I was

tired of feeling afraid in my own house.

When Tom called my name, I joined him downstairs. A massive branch had busted through a window in the living room, thanks to the storm. Tom said he could fix it. And while that was a relief, I was beginning to wonder who I should call to fix us.

Since it was the middle of the night, Tom covered the broken window with trash bags. It was the best he could do until morning. If we made it that far without another disaster.

He took me upstairs, but sex was off the table. His head was spinning, and so was mine. But we lay down in bed together and tried to sleep, listening to the rain outside.

"There's something I didn't tell you," he said.

"What?" I blinked several times. How could the night get any worse?

"When you went to the creek, I dug all the way to the bottom." He looked down and gnawed the inside of his cheek. "It wasn't there."

"What are you talking about?" I sat up in bed, beyond my limits of stress.

"The necklace," he mouthed. "We buried it six feet under. It's not there."

"Are you sure?" I asked. "I mean, it has to be."

"No." He grabbed my wrist. "It wasn't there, Addie. It's gone."

## Chapter 8

I woke up to the sound of a chainsaw.

In many ways, it was the least odd thing to happen in the past two days.

Exhausted from the night before, I rolled over and put a pillow over my head. That had to be the loudest chainsaw known to man. And it was quickly becoming the first inanimate object I wanted to kill.

"Uh!" I groaned, climbing out of bed. There was no point in trying to get any rest now. As if DeMilo wasn't a nightmare enough. Maybe it was better if I didn't sleep.

I never drank coffee, but I was about to start.

In the kitchen, I made a quick pot and nursed a whole cup to ease my pounding head. Tom must have been up for hours, slaving away in the summer sun. After last night, the living room was an utter disaster. Pieces of broken glass covered the carpet, and a branch large enough to rival a small tree dominated the room.

As Tom dragged the branch onto the porch, I headed outside to get an up-close look. He was wearing a white wife beater and his oldest pair of blue jeans. Despite the crisis, it was nice to see a Southern man breaking a sweat by my front door.

"Hey." He caught me staring and walked around the branch.

"I made a pot of coffee. Do you want some?"

"Thank you." He touched my shoulders as we kissed. "And yes."

Tom pulled me into his side as I leaned in for a hug. "Well, what do you think?"

"I can fix the window today." He pointed at the damage. "I've been sawing the wood into pieces, so it's easier to move."

"Yeah, I heard you," I teased. "It's a good thing I don't have neighbors."

"You do." He squeezed my waist and tapped my nose. "Me."

I giggled. "Let me get you some coffee."

"Wait." He pulled me into his arms and stole another kiss.

At the memory of last night, I touched his arm and shivered. "Tom?"

"Yeah, baby. What is it?" He tucked a lock of hair behind my ear.

"Will we ever be able to have a life? One day, just you and me? A family?"

"Come here." Tom patted my back and put

my head on his chest.

"I don't know what we're supposed to do. Should we call the police?"

"And tell them what? That the necklace we buried in the dirt has been stolen?"

I swallowed and picked at a snag in his shirt. "I'm scared."

"What good is being scared? I don't want to live like that anymore!"

"Yes, but you know what he's capable of," I stressed. "What if—?"

"Listen, I'll figure out a plan to get us out of here. Okay? Somewhere safe." He grabbed my hands and rubbed his thumb against my knuckles. "Don't you trust me?"

"Yes." I touched his arm when he caressed my face. "But he's your grandfather."

Every inch of his face turned rigid. "What is that supposed to mean?"

"I trust you," I muttered. "It's just that time before."

"He told me he was going to kill you! What choice did I have?"

I averted my eyes. "And now Daniel is dead."

That was the last straw. I shouldn't have said it. But there it was. Too late now.

"So I guess that's my fault, too." Tom wiped his dirty hands on a cloth and tossed it on the porch. Then he stomped inside and slammed the door. When it came to his behavior, I couldn't blame him. Because most of it was my fault.

We hardly said a word to each other the rest of the day, and I drove to Chateau Rogue alone. As I parked in front of Jeanine's house, the same feeling resurfaced. That strange sense of déjà vu I felt yesterday. Ricky was gone, but something about his presence was very much alive and well. In a way, he was still here.

I knocked on the front door, and Nicki walked out. Before I could say anything, she darted into the street. She looked so pale and thin in the sunlight. Like a ghost.

"Hey." Jeanine stood in the doorway. "Where's Tom?"

"A tree branch busted a window in the living room last night. He's at home fixing it."

"Oh." Her pretty blue eyes looked concerned. "The storm."

I nodded.

"Are y'all okay?" she asked.

There were so many ways to answer her question. With the truth? With a lie? Physically, my body had suffered no injuries. But my heart? My mind?

Between our fight and the prison break, I could hardly see straight.

I forced a smile and replied, "We're fine."

Since she was asking about our well-being, it really wasn't a lie. At least, that was what I kept telling myself as she welcomed me into the empty mansion. For a second, I wondered what it must be like to have a father who—on paper—was a billionaire.

Then again, my parents weren't that rich and they were never around. With the kind of money Lawton Travis was raking in, no wonder he was MIA in his own house.

"Want a brownie?" Jeanine pointed to a plate in the kitchen.

"Yes," I moaned, craving a chocolate fix. "Maybe more than one."

"Eat as many as you want." She opened the freezer and grabbed a pint of ice cream. "I made a double batch last night." As she dipped three scoops of mint chocolate chip, I felt something tug at my heart. She grabbed a spoon and cradled the bowl like a child.

"Jeanine, are you okay staying here overnight when your parents are gone?"

I followed her into the living room, where she plopped down on a leather couch. There was a coffee table in front of us covered with snacks. A bowl of Cheetos. A bag of M&Ms.

Despite her lavish upbringing, I felt sorry for her. Somehow, knowing she was in a billionaire's mansion in the suburbs sounded worse than when I stayed in the woods by myself.

"You know, you can always stay with me or Tom," I volunteered.

But she shook her head. "It's fine."

It was scary how much she sounded like me. Either she had too much pride to admit she was lonely and scared, or she was just so used to being neglected, that the thought didn't even register anymore.

Like Jeffrey and Eleanor. They were gone right now. But I didn't even care.

"Want to watch *Blood Diamond*? It was about to start before you got here."

"Oh, I forgot. The whole Leonardo DiCaprio marathon?"

"Oh my gosh, I'm having so much fun! I didn't go to bed last night until three."

Smiling at her excitement, I ate an M&M and said, "I'm glad."

No one wanted to take care of her, and she was making the best of it. I really admired Jeanine for that. Maybe she was stronger than I thought.

At least she'd had a better night than Tom and I had.

Once the movie ended, Jeanine turned the TV off and headed into the kitchen.

"Wanna go to the gym with me?" She sucked on a bottle of water like it was her dying breath. "I think I need to burn off all these calories. I could use the work out."

"Okay. Sure." I threw the plates and napkins in the trash. And Jeanine packed up the uneaten food, prancing around the place like a pony. "Umm..." I stopped her on her way out of the room.

Jeanine spun back as her hair flicked over her shoulders. She seemed wired.

"I don't have anything to wear." I looked down

at my jean shorts and flip flops. "My work out clothes—they're at home."

"Oh." She bit her lip. "You're probably the same size as Mom. You can just borrow some of hers." She took off up the staircase as I followed clumsily behind her.

"You're sure she won't mind? I mean, without you asking first?"

"No." She waved my question away with her hand. "She doesn't care."

When we reached the second floor, her words kept spinning around in my head. Almost like Jeanine was talking about more than her mother lending me clothes. Jeanine hadn't said, "She *won't* care." Maybe because the truth is always in the present tense.

Candy Travis didn't care, because she never had.

"Here." Jeanine handed me a pair of black athletic shorts with hot pink trim. Then she plucked a pair of tennis shoes from the closet along with socks and a Nike sports bra.

"Thanks." I held the clothes to my chest, wondering what was going on in her head.

"You can change in the bathroom." Jeanine led me down the hall and pointed to the end of it. "I'll be out in a minute." She walked into her room and shut the door.

Out of place, I started down the lengthy corridor looking from side to side. Despite our close friendship, I had never been upstairs in

Jeanine's house before. I had no idea where the bathroom was. And since every door was closed, I had to use trial and error to find the right one.

On my search, I found a laundry room, an office and a home gym. Flushed with embarrassment, I opened the next door and stepped inside. I needed to change clothes, and I guess it didn't really matter where that happened.

So I shut the door and set my borrowed clothes on the bed. As I looked around, movie posters caught the corner of my eye. Brad Pitt in *Fight Club*. Marlon Brando in *The Godfather*. I took a step closer and found football trophies with the words *Most Valuable Player* engraved in the finish. My heart pounded something fierce as it dawned on me.

I was in Ricky's room.

Everything looked just the same—as I imagined he had left it.

The doors to his closet were hanging wide open. His cologne still lingered on his clothes. A musky, urban scent that reminded me of grass and sweat. But maybe that was just the way he smelled.

His cleats were on the ground, and his backpack lay on the floor by the bed. I found his football jersey hanging on the headboard. TRAVIS was stitched across the back with the number fourteen beneath it. I picked up the jersey and took a whiff. It was freshly laundered, which made me empathize with Candy Travis like I never had before.

There were only two pictures in his bedroom. Each sat in black wooden frames on the nightstand by his bed. One featured a smiling Nicki in her cheerleader uniform. His arms were wrapped around her while she planted a kiss beneath the eye black on his cheek. It was taken after a football game, probably last season. And despite their volatile relationship, they both looked happy.

I pushed the picture frame aside to see the one hidden behind it.

And there it was—what I had feared most.

A photograph of me. My class picture from the ninth grade. I was only fourteen.

"Are you ready to-? What are you doing in here?" Jeanine stood in the doorway.

"Sorry." I turned around and stood in front of the picture. "I couldn't find the bathroom."

"It's down the hall." She pointed like she'd already told me.

"Oh, I'm sorry." I grabbed her mother's clothes with my head down.

"It's okay," she said. "You can change in here if you want to."

"I didn't mean to—I just."

Her dark blue eyes silenced me forever. Even though she was petite, I felt inferior to her when she walked into the room. "We haven't changed anything. It's all the same."

"That's good. I think he would like that."

Jeanine sat down on the bed. "I come in here sometimes and talk to him."

"I'm sure he likes that, too."

She smiled. "Do you think he hears me?" A tear rolled down her cheek.

I wrapped my arm around her. "Of course he does."

Jeanine broke down as I pulled her into a hug. For all intents and purposes, she was practically my little sister. Something that should have torn us apart had only brought us closer together. Ricky was her only brother. How could I hate her for missing him?

He was dead. And now she was an only child. Just like me.

For a long time, I couldn't understand it—why she didn't hate me.

Maybe she should.

"Why don't we go to the gym? And then we'll get some ice cream afterwards?"

She leaned back with a sniffle. "Doesn't that defeat the whole purpose?"

"Fine," I surrendered. "A nutritious, delicious smoothie instead."

"Sounds good." She stood up to dry her eyes. "Well, I'll let you change."

"Thank you." I slid out of my flip flops and pulled a pair of socks on.

"I'll be downstairs whenever you're ready." She shut the door behind her.

When Jeanine left, I changed into the work-out clothes she had given me. Mrs. Travis was a bit chestier up top than I was. Then again, I hadn't been put under while my boobs were sliced and filled with silicon. I shivered to get the painful image out of my head.

I looked at the pictures on Ricky's night stand one last time. It must have hurt Nicki for her boyfriend to keep my class photo so close by. Ricky wasn't the type to hide something like that from her. He was selfish to the core. He didn't care what she thought.

Ricky Travis was high-handed. In life, he had broken more hearts than I cared to know. In death, I can't say that he hadn't broken mine. Forever gone was the hope of him becoming a gentleman. When I had my first crush, all I had ever wanted was for Ricky to just be good, decent, kind. I would have given anything for him to be like Tom.

But he wasn't. Blood kin or not, he would never be like his cousin.

And now we were all paying the price for it.

We took a cycling class at the gym and then grabbed a fruit smoothie to cool off. As we made plans for the summer, I saw the many ways Jeanine favored her brother. Her skin was darker now that the seasons had changed, and those shiny black locks were just like Ricky's. They behaved like polar opposites. But they shared the same DNA.

And even though his actions were dishonorable, he must have loved his sister.

I hoped he had. Because his passing had put

her in a lot of pain. The absence of her parents multiplied the effect—her feelings of loss and isolation. I was used to parents who didn't care if you lived or die. For Lawton and Candy Travis, I guess it really was true.

On the way home, I thought about how lucky I was to have met Tom. Poor Jeanine was at home alone in that big mansion. And I knew she hadn't been sleeping at night.

That was why she stayed up until three in the morning watching Leonardo DiCaprio.

When I invited her to spend the night, she told me she would think about it. But I knew what that meant. She needed time to herself, time to think, time to be left alone.

So I gave her that. Even if she was safer sleeping under my roof with Tom around.

I parked at the end of the driveway and got out, searching for Tom. We hadn't left things the best this morning, but maybe that was my fault. Sometimes, we didn't know the right thing to say to each other. At least, not the right way to say it.

A huge branch lay in the yard—it had been sliced into smaller sections. I approached the wood, impressed that he had removed the limb from the window with his bare hands. Speaking of the window, Tom had already patched the hole for the night.

I walked inside and found him drinking a glass of water at the kitchen table.

"Hi." I took slow steps towards him and sat

down in the nearest chair.

"I called the hardware store, and they didn't have the right size window. These are custom." He pointed at the one in the kitchen. "So I ordered one, should be here next week."

"Thank you." I looked at the window. "You didn't have to do that, you know."

"It was no trouble, Addison." He stood up and rinsed his glass out in the sink.

Great. Now he was calling me *Addison* again.

"Why are you still so mad at me? What did I do?" I turned to face him.

"You really want to pick a fight with me? Now? It sounds like you're the one who's mad." He crossed his arms over his chest, and I noticed those large veins beneath his skin. Was he trying to intimidate me?

"I'm not mad." I held my hands in the air—my version of a white flag. "Why don't you let me pay you for fixing that window?" I reached for my purse. "There is no telling how much a professional would have cost."

"No." He shook his head, refusing my peace offering.

"Tom, please. It's the least I could do. My parents aren't even here. And if you hadn't been with me last night..."

He touched my hand, letting me know that the decision was final. "No."

When he walked off, I pushed my chair out and followed him. "So, listen, I've been thinking. I know last night was a bust, but what if we go back tonight? I watched this movie with Jeanine today, and it got me thinking."

He turned back, showing me that he was at least remotely interested.

"Well, what if it's close by? Maybe we picked the wrong spot."

"I thought the same thing." He ambled into the living room and sat down on the couch. "So I went back there today and dug up every square inch of that dirt. It's gone."

My heart sank to my gut. "What do you mean it's gone?"

"I mean, it's gone." He folded his hands and shrugged.

"*How* is it gone? Did they take it last night or—"

"Was it already gone when we got there? I don't know."

Panicking, I turned on my heel and headed for the door. "Well, I'm going out there."

Tom grabbed my arm. "No, you're not. It's not there, Addie. It's gone. Why won't you believe me?"

"Are you sure?" I cleared my throat. "You're sure you checked everywhere?"

"Well, not everywhere. But the only place it would be. What else can I do?"

I sank down to the floor and put my head in my hands.

"Breathe." Tom held on to my arm. "Why

don't you just calm down?" He headed into the kitchen and then came back. "Something came for you in the mail today."

With senior year approaching, I had been receiving solicitations from colleges all over the South East. Maybe it was related to that. I could handle that.

As he handed me the envelope, I searched his amber irises and held my breath. I flipped it over and read the back, raising my eyebrows. "It's from Atlanta."

"Maybe Georgia Tech," he guessed. "I got one, too."

I tore through the envelope as my eyes raced across the inside. "I already got one from Georgia Tech." When Tom squatted down, I handed him the letter.

"The Art Institute of Atlanta," he read. "Addie, you got in!"

"No." I snatched it back and skimmed the invitation. "It's an acceptance letter to their Summer Art Program. The one Caldwell wouldn't let me apply for."

"Well, that's great. Congratulations!" He leaned in to kiss me on the cheek.

"Tom." I touched his face. "I never sent in the application. How did I get in?"

"Maybe someone put in a good word for you." His fingertips lingered at my throat.

"Who?" I put my hand on his shoulder as he gazed into my eyes.

"Daniel?" It was weird not hearing him say Grandpa.

As I took a moment to process it, Tom planted a soft kiss on my lips.

"Atlanta," I sighed.

"Yeah." He rubbed my arm. "That's great, Addie."

I leaned to stand, and he helped me up.

"What is it?" He followed me into the kitchen, where I rifled through my purse.

I pulled out two tickets to see the Atlanta Braves and put them on his chest.

"Where did you get these?" Tom investigated further. "These are great seats."

"I found them today in Ricky's room. Jeanine wanted to go to the gym, so I changed in his bedroom. Before we left, there were a couple pictures on his night stand. When we got back, those were sitting beside the pictures. I don't know why I took them, I just—"

"When is the game?" he asked, looking down to check.

"Next week. The same time I would be there for the Art Institute."

Tom stared down at me. "It sounds like someone wants you in Atlanta."

"I know." I ran my fingers through my hair, nervously pacing the floor.

Tom put his hand on the small of my back. "I'm going with you."

"Maybe Jeanine should, too." I braided my

fingers at the nape of his neck, pulling him closer until our torsos were flush. "You know what's happening over here. Who do you think is going to her house and hiding in the bushes at night?"

"I guess you better get to packin' then," he drawled, sultry and sweet.

I tugged at his locks and slanted my mouth over his. As his hands raced up and down my back, I knew we would have to be careful on the road. Maybe it was a good thing Jeanine was coming along. That might be the only way to ensure I wouldn't get pregnant.

When I pulled away, Tom squeezed my hand and then slapped my butt. I ran up the stairs and looked back at him, winking as delicious heat rippled through me. In my bedroom, I grabbed a suitcase and tossed enough clothes inside for two weeks.

We were going to Atlanta. And I didn't know when we would be back.

# Chapter 9

I called Jeanine the night before, and we left bright and early the next day. We left a note for our parents. It was kind of ironic—now we were the ones ditching them.

See how they like coming home to an empty house.

You're never too old to get a taste of your own medicine.

When we reached Atlanta, I rolled down the window and stuck my head out. The skyline was amazing—buildings taller than trees. Concrete for grass. It was a forest of construction and commerce. Metal and reflective glass. And it was far enough away to make me forget about home. For now.

Tom pulled into the most expensive hotel he could find. As Jeanine led us through the revolving doors, I grabbed Tom's hand and put my lips on his. Even at fifteen, Jeanine carried herself with poise and confidence. When she approached the counter, my nails sank into the back of Tom's hand. But he told me to breathe.

"She's got this," he whispered, sliding his arm around my back.

Jeanine approached the front desk and slid an American Express Platinum Card across the counter. "I'll take two rooms please," she requested, cocking her head to the side.

We almost got laughed out of there until Jeanine pulled out her iPhone.

To my horror, she called her mother and father, who were spearing Alaskan salmon in the northern tip of Canada. "Jeanine, what are you doing?" I panicked at her audacity.

"Hi Daddy!"

I nearly fell over as Tom dragged me to a plush couch. "Is she crazy?"

"As weird as it sounds, I think she actually knows what she's doing," he said.

Waiting in suspense, I held my breath and watched her bat those long dark lashes. Within twenty minutes, she had secured two rooms on the sixteenth floor—and one of them had been upgraded to a suite. She strutted towards us in victory, distributing the keys.

"Who are you?" I laughed, while Tom gave her a round of applause.

"You're forgetting. My Daddy runs this town. And it's not just because he used to be a Falcon."

She snapped her fingers as bell boys hurried to get our luggage out of the car.

I turned to Tom, and he shook his head. "I think we've created a monster."

"So he didn't care? And they just let you right in?" I kicked my legs in the air as Jeanine lounged in the luxury suite. "When you called your parents, I thought the trip was over."

"Daddy knows the owner," she confessed.

"From football?" I assumed. "How?"

"He gave him the money to build the place."

I sat back against the plush pillows, relishing my silk bathrobe. "It's kind of a shame."

"What is?" She tied her hair back in a ponytail and then raided the mini-fridge.

"That our parents have built so much. I mean, your Dad is a former NFL player. Your Mom is a beauty queen. My Mom is a doctor. My Dad is a lawyer."

"Yeah, so..." She popped a bottle of ginger ale.

"Some people never have careers like that, never make that kind of money. Our parents are the cream of the crop. But I feel like I don't even know them."

"It makes sense." She stuck pink separators between her toes and then grabbed a bottle of blue nail polish. I had never seen her paint them anything non-traditional.

"What do you mean? That our parents ignore us?" I asked.

"Yeah." She shook the bottle of nail polish.

"More money for them."

"I'm sorry." I unzipped my suitcase to unpack, in awe of our room.

"For what?" Jeanine bit her lip as she painted her toenails, starting with the left.

"You're fifteen, and you drove to Atlanta without even asking permission. Then the hotel and this room." I knew she had already spent a fortune. "I just can't believe—"

"Well, they never ask my permission to do anything." She painted the nails on her right foot and then stood up, setting the bottle of polish down by the TV. "So they owe me."

"Why don't we split everything three ways? I feel bad that you're paying for it all."

"I told you, Daddy doesn't care. I've stayed at home by myself for years while they ran off and did whatever they wanted. I'm older now, and it's my turn to get what I want."

"Be careful," I warned, placing my shirts in a drawer.

She cocked her black brow at me, the anger and hatred boiling under the surface.

"I just don't want to see you getting into trouble."

"I won't," she assured me. "Come here. You're next."

Sprinting towards the rainbow of colors, I found a bottle of green polish and shook it. Jeanine nodded in approval and put some music on. The next thing I knew, she was ordering a buffet off the menu. I had never had room service like this before.

Someone knocked on the door, and I checked the peephole.

Beaming, I opened the door and Tom stepped inside. "That smells good."

I kissed him on the cheek as the door clicked shut. Then I fixed the chain just in case. Tom made a bee line for the gourmet entrées Jeanine had ordered.

"Help yourself, cuz," Jeanine twanged. "I'm takin' a shower."

As she slipped into the bathroom, Tom sliced into a steak and took a big bite. "Oh my God," he moaned through mouthfuls. "This tastes better than mine."

Pulling a cart in front of the bed, I sat down and shoved a bite of mac 'n' cheese down my throat. My eyes almost rolled into the back of my head. It *was* better than Tom's.

Everything was.

For the next half hour, we sampled everything from fettuccine alfredo to barbeque chicken pizza. There was vanilla ice cream with raspberries for dessert. Not to mention, a mountainous slice of chocolate cake. It was a good thing we had a fridge.

I wasn't about to let all this fine food go to waste.

"I'm stuffed." Tom lay across the bed with his hand on his stomach.

"Did you try the crab cakes?" I snuggled beside him. "They were to die for."

"Look at you," Tom chuckled. "An hour in a hotel suite, and you sound like a diva."

"Hey." I playfully knocked him in the shoulder. "I'm just saying, it was incredible."

"That's what she said," he quipped.

"Oh, shut up." I poked his ribs as we laughed. "You're just jealous."

"Why? Because they serve prime rib, and I've only given you brisket."

"You're the one that said their food was better than yours," I reminded him.

"Well, that's because it is." He put his hands behind his head and stared up at the ceiling. "I can't believe we're here in Atlanta. I've always wanted to take a trip with you."

"Really?" I sat up on my elbow. "Baby, that's so sweet," I chimed.

"So are you." His hand slithered around my back as he brought my mouth to his.

I put my head on his chest and sighed. "I'm worried about Jeanine."

"Why?" He ran his fingers through my hair. "She seems fine to me."

"You don't think it bothers her that she practically ran away from home, and her parents didn't even care? She's only fifteen. They should be more concerned."

"Look at your parents," he said. "They leave you in that house alone all the time. And you don't live in a subdivision like Jeanine. At least she has neighbors."

"I know, but—" I looked into his eyes. "It seems worse somehow."

"Because of Ricky?" He was so good at reading my mind.

"Well, yeah. If one of your kids was dead, wouldn't you keep an eye on the other one?"

"Just let her have fun." He stroked my arm. "We'll look out for her."

"Okay." I planted a kiss on his neck and then nuzzled closer.

When Jeanine got out of the shower, we watched movies until the sun set. Since we gorged ourselves during lunch, it took a while for an appetite to resurface. But when it did, I was eyeing the leftovers in the fridge like a lion at a river full of caribou.

"Why don't we go to The Varsity?" Jeanine said.

"Yes!" I hadn't been since I was a kid, but had fond memories of the place.

"The Varsity?" Tom sat up. "I don't think I've ever been there."

"You'll love it." I grabbed his arm and pulled him off the bed.

Jeanine slipped into her shoes and slid her purse over her shoulder. "Let's go."

On the way, I rolled the windows down and sang along to the radio. A new Taylor Swift song had just been released—one that was different for her. I heard she was getting a lot of flak for it, but I loved the beat. It made me want to do things I never had before.

When we arrived, the restaurant was packed. But Jeanine batted those lashes and got us a booth faster than I could blink. I squeezed in beside Tom and looked over his shoulder at the menu. He settled on a chili dog with fries, while Jeanine and I ordered hamburgers and onion rings. The waiter took our menus and left, and I snuggled closer to Tom.

It was so good to be away from everything in Savannah. I had always loved the woods, but I was embracing the concrete jungle. By the end of our trip, I would come to understand exactly why they called this place *Hotlanta*.

"So what's on the agenda for tomorrow?" Jeanine took a long sip of Coke.

"I'm going to the Art Institute and telling them that they made a mistake."

"What?" Jeanine practically had to yell over the crowd. "You got in, and you're just gonna walk in there and tell them, *No thank you. I'll pass*?"

"Yeah, Addie." Tom cradled my body in his arms. "Maybe you should reconsider. I mean, do you think they let everybody get in there?"

"If you do well, they may even offer you a scholarship," Jeanine said.

"There's no way." I shook my head. "I'm not that good."

"Addie?"

Recognizing my name, I looked up and found a pair of friendly blue eyes staring at me. I shook my head at the shock of seeing him, like a blast from the past I didn't see coming.

"Eric?" I got out of the booth and gave him a hug. "I haven't seen you in forever."

"I know." He patted my back and then held me at arm's length. "Wow, you've really grown up. What's it been? A few years?" he wondered.

"Yeah. Since you stood me up at the dance," I teased.

Eric rustled his blonde locks and blushed. "Yeah, sorry about that."

As we caught up, I looked him up and down. The last time I saw Eric, he was thirteen. Now he was sixteen and nearly six feet tall. He had filled out—chiseled and muscular with a sun-kissed complexion. My best friend's little brother wasn't so little anymore.

"So what are you doing in town?" he asked, stepping closer.

"Well, I got invited to the Art Institute for the summer," I beamed.

"Wow! Really? That's awesome." He rubbed my shoulder. "I remember you were always doodling in your notebook. I guess someone's been paying attention."

"Yeah." Tom stood up and wrapped his arm around my shoulder. "Someone has."

When I looked up, Tom was shooting daggers in my friend's direction. I had never seen his golden eyes look so dark. Almost black. The way Ricky's used to get.

"Eric, this is my boyfriend, Tom." I felt queasy as I made the introduction.

"Nice to meet you." Eric gave him a genuine smile and shook his hand.

"You too." Tom tugged at my waist until I returned to the table.

"Did you just get here?" I asked. "Why don't you sit with us?"

"Mom and Dad have a table in the back. It's kind of a work thing, but they let me tag along. I love the food here, but we don't come very often."

"Have you had the onion rings?" Jeanine piped up. "They're my favorite."

Eric noticed Jeanine for the first time and did a double take. "Hi."

I bit my lip, since he totally missed that she was asking him a question.

"Hi," she echoed, leaning into the wall. There was a giant space beside her.

"I'm Eric." He stuck his hand out, lingering over her touch. "What's your name?"

"Jeanine." She looked deep into his eyes and smirked—a dangerous influx of her lips. I had never seen her size up a guy until now. You would have thought he was her prey.

"Jeanine is Tom's cousin," I said. "And we're also really good friends."

"Really?" Eric nodded.

"Why don't you eat with us?" I asked. "Would

your parents mind?"

"I don't think so." He put his hand on the booth. "I haven't even ordered yet."

"We've got plenty of room." Jeanine motioned to the empty seat next to her.

"Okay." Eric squeezed into the booth and looked at a menu.

When our waiter returned, Eric placed his order and then looked around the table. I squeezed Tom's hand beneath the table, because I could feel his alpha male coming out. Sometimes, the fact that he was blood-related to DeMilo did scare me a little bit.

"So how do you two know each other?" Tom narrowed his eyes at Eric.

I rubbed Tom's arm and then braided my fingers through his.

"Eric and I went to school together. His family used to live in Savannah, but they moved to Atlanta a few years ago." I stared at Tom until he saw my eyes on him.

"Yep, that's about it. And our parents knew each other through work."

"Oh yeah. That's right." I had forgotten that part. "Eric's Dad is a surgeon and his Mom is an OBGYN. Just like mine." I shot Eric an innocent grin.

"It's funny bumping into you," Eric said. "I've been meaning to call. How are things in Savannah?"

I shared a silent exchange with Tom and

Jeanine. Widening eyes and knowing glances. But I blinked and scanned the table, returning my attention to Eric.

"Fine." I spotted the waiter with our food and breathed a sigh of relief.

As we passed plates around the table, Eric kept his eyes on me. I could feel it in the air—like a live wire. Eric was going to keep pushing Savannah until I told him everything.

To be honest, I should have known the questions would come. Eric must have heard about what happened. It wasn't like prom night hadn't been featured on the news.

"That's good." Eric leeched off a conversation I already thought was over.

Tom and I stared at Eric, hanging on every word he said.

"That things are better in Savannah, I mean." Eric took a modest bite out of his slaw dog and then wiped his mouth. "Because we're moving back."

I coughed on the air in my mouth. I hadn't even eaten anything yet. "What?"

Tom slapped my back as I struggled to get water down. I looked at Jeanine, and there were stars in her eyes. But she couldn't see what I could. The danger lurking near.

"Yeah. It will be nice to be home." Eric smiled, but he knew I wasn't happy.

"But I thought your Dad opened up a practice here," I said. "I thought business was better in

Atlanta. In the big city—more people and all that."

"Dad sold the practice." Eric nibbled at his fries. "And I'm sure they can find work in Savannah. Are you saying only people in Atlanta need doctors?"

"No." I wiped my clammy hands off with a napkin. "I just don't understand the rush to move back. I thought y'all were happy in Atlanta. Why are you moving back?"

"Because Savannah is home." He chewed on the ice in his drink. "We miss it."

Nodding, I bowed my head and played with my food. I wasn't hungry.

"Do you not want us to come back?" Eric asked. "I thought you'd be happy."

"Eric, I am happy. That's not it."

"Yeah, it sure sounds like you are." He got out of the booth and threw his napkin down. Jeanine watched him walk away, her blue eyes lingering on his silhouette.

"What was that about?" Jeanine pouted.

Turning to Tom, I nudged his shoulder and said, "I should go talk to him."

Tom chewed the inside of his cheek, pondering.

"Are you gonna let me out?" I held his amber gaze.

He took his time getting out of the booth. When Eric arrived, Tom had switched places with me. Now I knew why—so he could keep me trapped, away from the opposite sex.

"Thanks," I hissed, our bodies brushing on my way out.

When he grabbed my arm, I turned back with a scowl.

"Hurry back." He kissed the back of my hand—marking his territory.

Since the Varsity was packed. I had to fight and scratch my way through the crowd of customers and staff. When I spotted a sign pointing to the restrooms, I headed in that direction and waited. Eric never came out of the men's room, which led me to believe that he had never gone in there to begin with.

As the minutes ticked by, I searched for his parents at their table. It had been years, but I had a pretty good feeling they would recognize me. As children, Emily and I had been inseparable. It was only natural that her younger brother would become just as attached.

I know it sounds cliché, but we really were like the Three Musketeers. Even though Eric was a year younger than us, we had done everything together. As an only child, I had longed for siblings. So Eric and Emily became the brother and sister I never had.

"Eric!" I spotted a blonde head and followed it outside.

Eric loitered on the sidewalk, waiting for his parents. I couldn't believe he was sixteen already. Time goes by so fast. Despite what he thought, I really was happy to see him.

"Hey." I lowered my voice and touched his arm. "Eric."

"Yeah, it's nice to see you again, too," he grumbled. "I thought you would be happy."

"I *am* happy." I tugged at his shirtsleeve. "I'm just surprised is all."

Eric forgave me and rested his hand on my shoulder. "I've missed you."

"I've missed you, too." And it was the honest truth. He was like a brother to me.

With a sigh, Eric looked out at the city and slid his hands in his pockets.

"Do you like Atlanta?" I asked.

"It has its perks," he said. "But I miss the ocean and the trees."

"Savannah's not the place you remember."

Eric pinned his brows together, staring at the cars flying by.

"It's not safe," I warned. "Not anymore."

He shook his head and smoldered.

"What do you think I'm doing in Atlanta?" I asked.

It was a good point. If Savannah was safe, then what was I doing here?

Eric turned back to walk away. "I haven't forgotten what happened," he said.

I saw revenge in his eyes.

"Neither have I."

## Chapter 10

I don't know why you had to run him off," Jeanine scolded. "I liked him."

"I could tell." I stepped into the elevator and pressed the button to the sixteenth floor.

"Was it that obvious?" she asked.

"Yeah." Tom said. "I could see the drool from a mile away."

"What?" Jeanine wiped her mouth, smearing her lipstick in the process.

When I laughed, she glowered at us. Tom curled his elbow around my chest.

"Well, I thought Eric was friendly." She stuck her nose up in the air, ignoring us.

"A little *too* friendly, if you ask me," Tom said.

He tightened his arm around my neck, aligning my back with his chest.

"Are you jealous?" I teased, pinching his cheek.

"Maybe." He lowered his head and slanted his mouth over mine.

"Eww... Get a room!" The doors parted, and Jeanine stomped out.

Tom grabbed my hand and pulled me down the hall. "We've already got one!"

She let herself into our suite and slammed the door.

"Maybe we shouldn't be so rough on her," I sympathized. "She has a crush."

"So do I." He kissed me, and I felt it everywhere.

Fluttering my lashes, I lifted my chin and leaned towards him. Tom brushed the back of his knuckles against my neck as his mouth landed on mine. Lost in sensation, I wrapped my arms around him until our bodies were flush. He stumbled backwards, molding his hands to the curves of my face. I was panting and breathless, flustered with heat.

Tom turned to the side and unlocked the door, pushing me into his room. All of the lights were off, and I had no intention of turning them on. When the door clicked shut, Tom grabbed my head and kissed the corner of my mouth. His aim was off, but I didn't mind.

Walking backwards, I grabbed his elbows to steady myself. His fingers sliced through my hair, as we stumbled in the darkness. When I reached for his shirt collar, Tom cradled his arm around my back and pulled me in close. I touched his cheek and whimpered.

"I love you." His nose trailed my neck as he pressed a kiss below my ear.

*Love.* A word we had used and felt often. But never acted on.

What if he wanted to *love* me? What if he wanted to *show* me? Right now.

I pushed him into a chair and ran my fingers through his hair.

"Addie." He watched me looming above him, a desperate plea in his eyes.

He took my hands and put them on his face. Forced to take a step closer, I ran my thumb against the stubble on his cheek and shivered. Tom looped his arms around my waist while his eyes stayed on me. My knees grew weak as he tugged, pulling me into his lap.

I put my hands on his shoulders and then circled them at the nape of his neck. His hands roamed up and down my back as we held each other closer, chest to chest.

"Hi," I whispered.

He hugged me and brushed the tip of his nose against mine. "Hi."

Smiling at the touch of his lips, I feathered my fingers through his hair. Tom leaned back in the chair as I sat down between his legs. All space vanished between us.

Kissing him felt so right. When he touched me, I forgot about where we were or why we were here. It was just me. Just Tom. Tempting each other in the night.

In the protection of his arms, I felt exempt from all harm. His body was a safety net. Locking me up tight. Away from the dangers of the world. Away from fear. And death.

I tilted my head back as he kissed my neck. Sweet, delicate touches. He was tender and attentive—cultivated by years of waiting. Years of longing. Years of yearning.

I curled my arm around his shoulder and lifted his chin. Tom looked like a sick puppy. In need of tender loving care. So I covered his mouth with a sweet kiss—not knowing where it would lead— and he tightened his grip.

Tom tugged at the back of my neck and took his time cherishing my lips. Like they weren't something to be tasted, but *savored.*

His hand slid up my shirt, and I knew we were dancing on a tight rope. But the tips of his fingers felt like honey on my skin—soft and sweet. I tangled my fingers through his hair and relished the kiss, committing it to memory.

When Tom reared back, I held my breath and watched him drag his shirt over his head. He struggled with the sleeves, so I pulled at the fabric until it hit the floor. Those golden eyes traced a line from my hair to my mouth.

Tom was admiring me. And from the look of it, he liked what he saw.

My heart beat like a drum, and I felt so hot I could scream. But Tom swept a lonesome lock behind my ear, dragging his thumb down my throat. Closing my eyes, I absorbed the sensation and searched for breath. Was this what it was like? *Sex?*

We hadn't even started yet. Part of me was scared to. I didn't know if I could handle it.

Tom took a breath and bit the corner of his mouth. As his hands settled at the small of my back, I leaned into the chair and sighed. My eyes drifted down as I searched the beautiful marble that was his body. *Smooth skin. Hard lines. Rugged muscle.*

The fire between us spread, and I thought it might scorch me to the bone. He stroked his thumb across my bottom lip. It was so hot, I shivered.

"Addie," he crooned darkly.

But I was helpless.

"What are we doing?" He cupped my cheeks and stared at my face.

I didn't know. Maybe that was why they called it the *point of no return.*

"Are we really about to...?"

Right then, I made up my mind. All these mixed up feelings had turned me wishy-washy. But a change of scenery had made everything crystal clear.

Tom loved me. And we could use protection. We could be safe.

We lived in an evolved time—one that let you break the rules without all the risk. If any part of me were in danger, it wasn't my body. It was my heart.

And Tom had that cradled in the palm of his hand.

So the only question left... What was I waiting for?

We had been interrupted so many times before. Three if I was keeping count. But there was no way our intimacy could be denied now. Running off to Atlanta was the perfect solution to a blissful summer in his arms. And if the night continued, in his bed.

"What if we are?" I curled my hands around his neck and lowered my head. My hair surrounded us like a veil, and I felt exactly what intimacy is meant to be. *Close.*

Would I ever have him close enough? Maybe there was a way to finally find out.

His fingers danced across my face as I closed my eyes, bringing my mouth to his.

Before our lips touched, someone banged on the door and I froze.

Tom squeezed my leg with a groan. "I am going to kill whoever is behind that door."

"Addie? Tom?" Jeanine cried. "Addie? Addie, are you there?"

"Yeah," I called out. "What is it?"

As I listened, Tom planted a kiss on my neck and tightened his hold.

"Addie," Jeanine cried, sending fear straight through my veins. Sharp and searing.

I went to climb out of Tom's lap and he grabbed my body. "No," he growled.

"I need to see if she's okay." I pushed off his shoulders and stood up. "It will only take a second." When he grumbled, I turned back and said, "She's *your* cousin."

Jeanine kept knocking on the door and twisting the handle. I had never seen her so impatient. So I unfastened the latch and opened the door, surprised to find what I saw.

"Are you okay?" I took a step back to let her inside.

She looked cold and pale, crying with streaks of mascara down her cheeks. As I stood in the doorway, she glanced over her shoulder, staring down the hall. Tom put his shirt back on and walked up behind me to see what all the fuss was about.

"Jeanine, what's wrong?" I put my hand on her shoulder, but she wouldn't move. It was the strangest thing—the way her body felt solid as stone.

Tom leaned against the wall as we waited for her to say something, anything.

I put the back of my hand to her forehead, and it was clammy. She crossed her arms over her chest and shivered. But her eyes remained in the hallway, her head turned.

Jeanine was known for her bright eyes—as blue as the night is dark. But the light had gone out in them. Not just faded or dimmed. *Gone.* Like someone had crept inside her and flipped the switch. She was a candle without the flame.

"You look like you've seen a ghost," I said.

It was an accurate assessment. She wasn't just scared. Jeanine was *terrified*.

"I-I-I. Umm." She licked her lips and broke down crying. "I think I saw—"

Tom huddled closer and I furrowed my brow, wondering what lay at the end of the hallway. She stared in that direction and covered her mouth, sobbing uncontrollably.

Whatever she saw was making me nervous. So I pulled her into the room and comforted her like the little sister I never had. Tom rubbed her back and then looked me in the eye, seeking approval for the one thing I didn't want him to do.

He stepped into the hall and looked both ways. Not knowing what was out there made fear all the more unwelcome. But Tom was never afraid. Maybe not of anything.

Once Jeanine sat down on the bed, I popped outside the door to keep an eye on Tom. For the life of me, I couldn't figure out what Jeanine had seen. Tom explored every inch of the sixteenth floor and then came back to me.

"Did you find anything?" I asked.

"No." He shook his head. "Nothing."

"Jeanine seems pretty spooked. Maybe we should all stay in your room tonight."

Tom squeezed my shoulder and touched my hair. "Okay."

He kissed my head and then pulled me into his arms. I buried my face in his chest and squeezed tight, wishing I could hold on to him forever. I felt like a fool, because I thought Atlanta was our safe haven. Instead of escaping the past, we had brought it with us.

I never could get Jeanine to tell me what she saw. After she fell asleep, I went back to the suite and collected our things. Jeanine slept like a starfish in the middle of the bed. So I dropped her bags on the floor and sank into a chair.

Throwing my head back, I shut my eyes and sighed. I thought about what Tom and I almost did in this chair—things that could not be undone. He may have been patient for his age, but how long could my boyfriend stand the temptation? The burning desire?

"I'll sleep on the floor."

My eyes shot open as I sat up straight. Tom spread a blanket on the floor and tossed a spare pillow onto it. His eyes met mine, and I watched him strip down to his boxers.

Blood sang hot and loud beneath my skin. But Jeanine was in the room, and that was the only thing that kept me from pouncing like a lioness. I looked at her on the bed—hogging the whole thing—and wondered where I would sleep.

"Good luck with that." Tom lay down and tucked his hands behind his head.

Fighting a grin, I watched Jeanine snore and then set my sights on Tom. "There are only two pillows in this room." I made my way towards him. "And you have the second one."

Tom cocked his head to the side and grabbed my leg. "Well, why don't we share it?"

I looked back over my shoulder to make sure Jeanine was asleep.

"She's out," he said. "Come on, I don't bite."

"Let me change first." His hand fell from my leg as I headed to the bathroom. After slipping into a long t-shirt and pajama shorts, I splashed cool water on my face and brushed my teeth. I looked in the mirror and thought about Jeanine, what she saw.

Maybe it was nothing. But I bolted the lock on the door. Just in case.

Jeanine was sound asleep. And when I crept back to Tom, he was too. So I slid beneath the blanket and lay down beside him. Even now, I couldn't believe how beautiful he was. He had a baby face and pouty lips. And yet, looked every bit of the man he was.

I touched the stubble on his face and then put my head on his chest. There was a heart beneath the muscle and bone. I never imagined that one day, it would stop beating.

As I shut my eyes, Tom rubbed my arm and drifted off.

I fell asleep to the sound of his breath in my ear.

## Chapter 11

On Monday morning, I wrestled in the traffic of downtown Atlanta. My acceptance letter to the Art Institute had clearly been a mistake. How could I be in the summer art program when I had never even applied for it? Sure, it had been an aspiration of mine. One that Principal Caldwell had squashed months ago.

Tom dropped me off at the front door, while I looked up at the building. It was all black windows—about as tall as they were wide. Now that I was here, it was just a place. Even though I had an acceptance letter, I no longer felt the excitement I had once harbored for the institute. Because I knew that I hadn't earned the right to be here.

I stood at the entrance, wondering if I should even go in. Would it be better to never show up at all? Someone touched my hand, and I looked back to find Tom behind me.

"I thought you were going to the Coca-Cola Factory with Jeanine?" I said.

"Not yet," Tom muttered. "I want to take you with me."

"Tom, I've seen a bottle of Coke a million times. Y'all can go without me."

"Yes, but have you tasted all the flavors? They have Coke from every country."

Cradling my back in his arms, Tom searched my face and I smiled. "I think this is something that I need to do by myself. And what about Jeanine?"

"She wanted to stay in the car." He took my hand and led me to the entrance. "Come on. I'll wait in the lobby if you don't want me going in there with you."

I dragged my feet in an attempt to resist him, but Tom got his way in the end.

"Tom, I don't know how long this is going to take," I insisted. "You'll just get bored."

"No, I won't." He tapped the end of my nose and dragged me after him.

Cold air hit me the minute we walked inside. I had an icy introduction to the place but it was a pleasant relief from the blistering heat outside. But just as much of a shock to my system. There was a receptionist at the front desk. And she seemed friendly enough.

"Hi." I approached her while Tom lingered over my shoulder.

"What can I help you with today?" Her blonde hair was short and neat. She wore a silk blouse and a minimal amount of makeup—just enough to look semi-professional.

"I got this letter in the mail." I leaned on the counter as I handed it over. "It's for the summer art program. But I never applied, so this must be a mistake."

She skimmed the acceptance letter and set it aside. "Let me look you up in the system."

"Thank you," I breathed a sigh of relief.

As she tapped my name out on her keyboard, I looked back at Tom. He was walking around the lobby with his head in the clouds, staring up at the high ceilings. There was a spiral staircase fit for a queen that led to the floor above us. Even now, with my hopes set on leaving this place, I wondered what was up there.

"Addie Smith?" The receptionist handed the letter back.

"Yes." There was a stern look on her face. It felt like I was in trouble.

"You are currently enrolled in the program." She clicked the mouse as her eyes flitted over the computer screen. "But you missed orientation and today's first session."

"Okay." I furrowed my brow with a pout. "How do I drop the program?"

Her eyebrows shot to the ceiling, and I knew I had said the wrong thing.

"It's just that I never applied to the program," I

repeated. "I didn't even find out I got in until the last minute. And I would hate to take someone else's spot."

"Do you have any idea how few students we accept? How hard it is to even be considered?" She took out an emery board and shaped the end of her nails.

"Sure, but I never applied. I've told you that twice now."

Tom perked up at the change in my voice and stood beside me.

"So, I guess what you're saying is, you don't want to be here."

"No." I shook my head. "I'm not *supposed* to be here."

Tom put his hand at the small of my back, and I pushed it away. Now was not the time for soft touches and flattery. When the receptionist turned her head, I bit my tongue and glared. She slid a piece of paper across the counter and put a pen on top of it.

"Fill out this form and take it upstairs. You'll need the Art Director to sign off."

"Okay." I looked her in the eye. "Thank you."

She averted her gaze and answered a phone call, while I found a seat in the lobby.

Tom sat down beside me, watching my every move. "I'm sorry."

"It's okay." He lowered his voice so it wouldn't echo. "I know how stressed you get."

I reached out and touched his hand. "Thank

you."

When our eyes met, I knew he had forgiven me. That was Tom. He wasn't known for turning the other cheek. Unless the inflictor was someone he truly cared about.

Once the form was complete, I went up to the receptionist and gave her the pen back. Since she was on the phone, I couldn't ask her for further instructions. So I nodded at Tom and we ascended the staircase together, looking down at the cold lobby below.

"Where do you think the Art Director is?" I asked.

"In his office?" Tom led me down the hall, and I saw it as a protective gesture. I could be so cruel to him sometimes. His unconditional love made me want to be sweeter.

"Or *her* office," I corrected. "What makes you so sure the Art Director isn't a woman?" I held the form to my chest and stared him down.

"It's on that." He pointed at the form. "I don't know many women named James."

"Oh." I scanned the form until I saw the name James Blake.

"Here we go." Tom pointed to a door at the end of the hall. "Is this him?"

There was a name plate with Dr. James Blake on the door. "I guess so."

All of a sudden, my heart started pounding. I don't know why I got so nervous. But I felt like a coward, barging into the Art Director's Office to ask permission to leave.

"Why don't you just knock?" Tom hovered, breathing down my neck.

"Stop. Rushing. Me." Each word came out like a military command.

Tom widened his eyes and took a step back. Somehow, being in this place had me so on edge that I couldn't handle the slightest push forward. Even if it was in the right direction.

With a shallow breath, I lifted my hand and rapped my knuckles against the door. There was no commotion on the other side. After a moment of silence, I knocked again.

"Maybe he's not in there." Tom shoved his hands in his pockets and shrugged.

I tried the handle, but the door was locked. "I'll just stand here and wait."

Down the hall, a class let out as a handful of students spilled into the corridor. Once they cleared out, I found the door hanging wide open and entered the room. While I knew nothing about interior design, the space looked nothing like a classroom.

At Maple Creek High, it was old wooden desks and plain carpet. But here, there were glass walls and leather swivel chairs. I spotted a few throw pillows in the corner, and a moveable white board up front. It was modern and stylish, attractive.

I crept deeper into the room and felt like an intruder. Sunlight poured in from the west, and I smiled at the window. Something about this room felt special, sacred. I had glimpsed the other classrooms in the hall. And they looked nothing like this.

"Can I help you?"

My head snapped up at the sight of a man. He was standing at the front of the room, tucked behind the white board. Once he moved it out of the way, I got my first real look at him.

He must have been in his forties. Dark eyes. Salt 'n' pepper hair. Rough face.

"Hi, umm." I clutched the form in my hand. "I'm looking for the Art Director."

"What is it that you need?" He put a few books away and then came towards me.

He took long strides and dominated the room, holding his hand out. I felt nervous and clumsy as I showed him the form. He was in my face before I was ready for him.

"Sorry to bother you," I said. "Do you know where he is?"

"Hmm." He leaned back against the table and frowned. "So you want to drop the summer art program? Care to give me a reason why?"

His dark eyes settled on me, and I couldn't find the words.

"Why don't you have a seat, Miss—Smith—is it?"

"Yes sir." I sat down in front of him, while he hovered above me.

"So, it says here you're from Savannah." His eyes flicked to the form.

"Yes." I looked around the room to see if Tom was still here and breathed a sigh of relief when he was.

"I wonder, why come all this way when a simple phone call would have sufficed?"

"What?" I cleared my throat. "I mean, excuse me?"

"You drove five hours to fill out a form?" He raised a dark eyebrow, putting me on the spot.

"Well, that's not the only reason why I'm in Atlanta."

"Oh?" He turned his attention to Tom.

"I never applied for the summer art program. That's why I would like to drop it. So if you could let me know where the Art Director is, I'll be out of your hair."

He gave me a passive smile and then signed his name on the form.

"Oh, I'm sorry." I blushed in embarrassment. "I didn't realize—"

"You can call me Jimmy." He stuck out his hand for me to shake.

"Thanks Jimmy." I took the form when he gave it to me. "I appreciate it."

I turned around and headed for the door, smiling at Tom in the back.

"Are you an artist, too?" Jimmy asked, setting his eyes on Tom.

"No, that's just Addie." Tom put his arm around my shoulder.

"Tom is a singer-songwriter," I bragged. "He

plays the guitar, too."

"We have an open mic night," Jimmy said. "You're welcome to perform."

"Thanks, but I'm not sure how long we'll be in Atlanta," Tom replied.

"We should probably get going." I grabbed his hand and squeezed.

"Addie," Jimmy called after me. "I'd be curious to see your work."

His interest surprised me, but was not wholly unwelcome.

"To be honest, I haven't picked up a paint brush in months," I confessed.

"Well, that's a shame." He led us out the door. "Let us know if you change your mind."

"Thanks." I dragged Tom behind me, in a rush to get out of there. Until I saw the paintings hanging in the hall. I had been so distracted before, I hadn't even noticed.

Jimmy passed us and went into his office. Since we wouldn't be back, I took the time to admire each piece of art. Some were abstract, some still life, some watercolor. I loved how the institute welcomed difference with open arms. No judgement or criticism.

Art is subjective. And I saw the beauty in every painting. Where a portrait examined individuality, a landscape explored the vast unknown. I spent my time on each one, thankful that Tom was letting me. But then I saw a watercolor that stopped my heart.

It looked like the mansion—where Tom lived, where Daniel had. The white columns blended into a body of water and trees surrounded the house—the only source of green in the painting. There was blue and subtle shades of violet, not strictly cool colors.

Upon closer inspection, I found a splotch of red hidden in the painting. I suppose it could have been misplaced, an accident maybe. But then I realized where it was.

A pool of blood on the doorstep.

Something came over me and wouldn't let go. Like a sudden dose of poison. I was infected with it—the need to grab that painting and run.

"Addie, what are you doing?" Tom followed me down the hall.

I barged into Jimmy's office and said, "I want to buy that painting."

Jimmy cocked his head to the side, not at all surprised to see me again. "Okay."

"How much do you want for it?" I opened my purse. "I'll write you a check."

"Addie." Tom grabbed my arm. "This is crazy."

Jimmy got out of his chair. "Which painting?"

"The watercolor." Together, we walked back into the hall.

With his hands in his pockets, Jimmy took a good long look at the painting in question. "Why this one?" He turned his head and looked right through me.

"No reason." I gulped, knowing I was a bad liar.

"Well, you'll have to take a second look. That one's not for sale."

I caught his elbow when he started to walk away. "Why not?"

Jimmy stared at my hand on him, and I withdrew it in shame.

"Because it's not for sale."

I stood with my mouth gaping open as he went into his office and shut the door.

"On a scale of one to ten, how stupid was that?" I asked.

Tom stood behind me, his breath on my neck. "An eleven."

"What is wrong with me?" I ran down the staircase as Tom hurried to catch up.

When we reached the lobby, I handed my form to the receptionist. She gave me the green light, and I was officially dismissed from the summer art program. Tom took my hand and led me into the parking lot where Jeanine was waiting.

As he dragged me to the car, I held my breath and looked back.

Jimmy was watching me through his office window.

## Chapter 12

This is amazing!" Jeanine took another sip of Cherry Coke. "Do you think they'd let me move in?" Her lips were stained red, but it wasn't from her lipstick.

"You two need to slow down." I crossed my arms over my chest, refusing to enjoy our time at the World of Coca-Cola. It was a place none of us had ever been. Even Jeanine, which surprised me since her dad had been an Atlanta Falcon for all those years.

"You're such a buzz kill." Tom refilled his cup and clinked it with Jeanine's.

Rolling my eyes, I strolled over to a drink station without a care in the world. To be honest, I didn't want to be here. And the fact that I couldn't get that not-for-sale watercolor out of my head didn't help much. I wanted that painting because it reminded me of Daniel.

And all the reasons why he was no longer with us.

Tom snuck up behind me and pressed the rim of his drink to my lips. Resisting, I dug my elbows into his chest and hated that I couldn't enjoy this. For some reason, I couldn't get what had happened at the Art Institute out of my head.

"Fine," I succumbed, sucking down every last drop.

As I wiped my mouth, Tom and Jeanine stopped and stared.

"What was that?" I held the cup up to see through the bottom.

"Fanta." Jeanine watched me like she couldn't believe it.

"That was good." I nodded at them. "I want more."

Tom chuckled and came after me, hot on my heels. For the next hour, I gave him my full attention. I could tell he was having the time of his life, and it would help if I would have it with him. So we walked hand in hand, sampling saccharine until we were dizzy.

As the afternoon carried on, I let my earlier disappointment fade. We visited the theatre and then took a picture with the Coca-Cola Polar Bear. He was warm and fluffy, but way cooler than a mascot at a football game.

When the sun set, Tom wrapped his arm around me and sealed the day with a kiss. In that moment, I wanted to be fully present with him.

But it was hard to do.

Looking back, I should have appreciated how much he loved me. I was spoiled—having Tom as my first and only boyfriend. But his goodness and affection was eclipsed by fear.

If we ever made it back to Savannah, I knew what was lurking in the darkness. Waiting for me. I wasn't ready for it. But when it came to mind, I also wasn't ready to let it go.

Back at the hotel, we were still buzzing from our sugar rush. I yawned and leaned my head into Tom's shoulder. He pulled me close, and I loved his strength and warmth.

"Did you have fun today?" he whispered in my ear.

"Yeah." I kissed him and felt his smile on my lips. "Did you?"

Tom nodded and squeezed my waist, eliminating the space between us. For a second, my heart did a little leap. I thought about what happened last night and wondered if we were headed down the same path. Would it be so bad if we did? Did I want to?

Jeanine pushed the button for the elevator, and it opened. Her mouth hit the floor when the doors parted and Eric stepped out. I blinked twice, totally confused.

"Eric?" I made room for him in the hallway. "What are you doing here?"

"My parents are here for a medical conference. Mom left something at the house and wanted me to bring it. What about y'all? You stayin' in this hotel?"

"Yep." I nodded, happy to see my old friend again. "We just got back from the World of Coca-Cola."

"Oh, really?" He played with his car keys. "Have you ever been before?"

"Nope, first time. For all of us, actually."

Eric smiled at Jeanine and she just stood there. For someone who never shut up, I couldn't understand why she had gone mute. Especially since she had loved the factory even more than us. That polar bear had a number one fan now, and it was her.

"Did y'all like it?" Eric had included all of us, but he was only looking at Jeanine.

"Yeah," I finally said—because she wouldn't. "We loved it."

"How about you?" He waited for Jeanine to answer, and I couldn't stand the tension. So I shot daggers at her and mouthed, *Say something.*

"You've got something on your face." Eric swiped his thumb across her cheek, and I thought she was going to faint. When she kept quiet, he shoved his hands in his pockets and took a step back. "Well, I better get going. I'll see you guys later."

"Bye." I waved as he left through the lobby.

Jeanine pined for him like a sick puppy, watching him walk away.

As soon as the elevator doors closed, I grabbed

her by the arm. "What the hell was that?"

"What?" She crossed her arms over her chest and leaned against the wall.

"Eric is clearly into you."

"I don't know." She tucked a lock behind her ear and clung to her purse. "I don't think so. He was just being nice." Warm blush splattered across her cheeks and I sighed.

"Jeanine, I've known Eric my whole life. Trust me, he's into you."

When my cell phone vibrated, I pulled it out of my purse. "Oh. It's Eric."

Jeanine held her breath, hanging on my every word as I talked to him. When I got off the phone, she stared me down, squeezing every last drop of truth out of me.

"His car won't start." I dropped my phone into my purse. "So I told him to come up."

"He's coming to the room?" Tom watched the floor number change. "Great."

"What is wrong with you?" I slapped his arm. "Why are you so jealous?"

Tom put those honey colored eyes on me. "He can be a little too friendly."

"Ugh." I shut my eyes in frustration. "Tom, Eric is like a brother to me. Ask him. I'm sure he'll say the same thing."

We stepped off the elevator, and I moved my suitcase back into the suite.

"What are you doing?" Tom caught my arm in the hall.

"Jeanine isn't spooked now. So we're gonna stay in the suite."

Tom let go of me and nodded, turning to walk away.

"Where are you going?"

"I'm gonna take a shower. Then maybe we can all go out for dinner."

"Okay." I watched him leave as Jeanine passed me in the hall.

Back in our suite, I forgot about the reason why we had left. Jeanine sat on the bed and grabbed the remote, searching for a Leonardo DiCaprio movie on TV. As I unpacked my things, she lowered the volume and ran a brush through her hair.

"Tell me about Eric," she said. "What's he like?"

"Well, I was best friends with his sister growing up. And Eric was in the grade below us. He's really sweet and smart. Pretty mature for his age, actually."

"How old is Eric?"

"Sixteen." I opened the closet and looked over my shoulder at her. "A year older than you."

"So, if he's like a brother to you, does that mean you trust him?"

I smiled at her questions. What was she getting at?

"Yeah, totally. Eric is a great guy."

Jeanine nodded, thinking everything over. "You really think he likes me?"

152

"Yes." I slid my shirts onto hangers. "I really do."

"Because, well when we first saw him, I sort of thought he liked you."

"Why don't I do this?" I sat down on the end of the bed. "I'll talk to him and find out if I'm right."

"No!" Jeanine sat up in a panic. "You can't tell him I like him."

"I'm not going to." I tied my hair back in a ponytail. "Trust me."

"Okay." She bit her lip and smiled. "Because I do like him."

"That's good." I put my suitcase away and shut the closet doors.

"I mean, he's gorgeous. He kind of looks like Leonardo DiCaprio."

I saw *Titanic* on the TV screen and watched the actor in question sinking with the ship. "Umm... I don't really see it. But I guess so."

While there was no obvious resemblance, Eric did have blonde hair, blue eyes and a good looking face. Maybe that was all Jeanine had meant. Not to mention, the killer smile.

There was a knock on the door, and I looked through the peephole. "It's Eric."

"Okay." Jeanine leapt out of the bed. "What do I do?"

"Just breathe," I instructed. "Act natural."

"Okay." She nodded. It seemed like the only word she knew how to say.

I opened the door for Eric. "Hey! Come in."

Eric walked into the room, and it was palpable—Jeanine's nerves. Her eyes were glued to the TV screen. And for once, I knew it had nothing to do with her celebrity crush.

"So what's up with your car?" I asked.

"I don't know." He ran his fingers through his hair. "I'm thinking it's the battery."

"Well, we could try to jump it off. But I don't know if Tom has any jumper cables."

Eric nodded, but the TV distracted him. And then his eyes were on Jeanine.

"Jeanine, do you know if Tom has jumper cables in the car?" I asked.

"Umm... I don't know." She stared at the screen. "You could ask him."

I leaned into Eric with a laugh. "Don't expect anything out of her as long as *Titanic* is on. When it comes to Leonardo DiCaprio, she's kind of obsessed."

"Hey!" Jeanine gave us her full attention. "I heard that."

"It's okay," Eric replied. "He's a great actor."

Jeanine looked Eric up and down, and it was a sight to behold. For a second, I thought she might rip his clothes off. As they stared at each other, I took my cue to leave.

"I think I'll go ask Tom about the jumper cables," I told Eric.

"Okay." He nodded at me and then sat down in a chair by the window.

"And why don't you come to dinner with us tonight? While you're stranded here."

He looked at Jeanine for her approval, and she didn't object. "Okay."

"Okay," I echoed. Apparently, it was the only word any of us could say. "Let me go check on Tom, and I'll be right back."

I walked out the door and hoped it was all right that I was leaving them alone together. Clearly, they needed to get a few points across. Like the fact that they were both foaming at the mouth for each other. Even though neither was willing to admit it.

When I got to Tom's room, I knocked on his door and it opened. I found it odd that he wouldn't lock the door before jumping in the shower. But didn't think anything of it.

"Tom?" I shut the door and stepped inside. All the lights were off, and I didn't hear the shower running. The door to the bathroom was cracked, so I walked into the hotel room.

Two baseball tickets lay on the table by the window. I had taken them from Ricky's room and wondered if Jeanine would hate me for it. The Atlanta Braves were playing tomorrow afternoon. But I knew we couldn't go. It just felt wrong.

As I walked past the bathroom, Tom opened the door and pulled me inside. I squealed when his arms went around my waist and he lifted me onto the counter. His hair was wet, and there was a white towel around his waist. The only thing covering him up.

He kissed me on the mouth and then dragged his lips down my throat. I shut my eyes and forgot how to breathe, digging my nails into his back. "Tom, I need to ask you—"

"Yes." He threaded his fingers through my hair and kissed the corner of my mouth.

"You didn't even let me ask the question," I complained.

"Answer's still yes." His hand settled at the small of my back.

"Tom, we need to focus," I sighed, digging my fingers into his neck.

"Okay?" He put his hands on the counter. "What do you want to ask me?"

I looked at his face and forgot my own name.

He touched the furrow between my brows and leaned in, blanketing me with warmth. Before I knew it, his mouth was on mine, and I just couldn't say no. Not this time.

His hand slid up my thigh and I leaned my head back. Part of me needed the distance, almost like I couldn't decide if I wanted to run away. But then he buried his face in my neck, and I didn't know how we had made it this long without sealing the deal.

I curled my legs around his waist and gave in to temptation. All the times spent fighting it, I should have known it would come to this. We were alone in a hotel room in Atlanta.

In that moment, I trusted Tom so much. With

my heart, my body, my soul.

I never thought he would lie to me.

When he picked me up in his arms, I wrapped my body around him. He covered my face with kisses and almost tripped on our way to the bed. Once he put me down, I tugged at the back of his neck until he was dangerously close.

He kissed me like he never had before and someone screamed.

Tom froze above me and I gasped, waiting for the other shoe to drop. I heard cries from the hallway and pushed him off me. As Tom put his clothes on, I ran out of the room and found the door to our suite hanging wide open.

To my surprise, no one had stepped into the hall to see what the ruckus was about. My heart was hammering in my chest as I put one foot in front of the other. Tom was hot on my tail, brushing past me and into the hotel room.

We found Jeanine on the floor with Eric crouched down beside her. I looked around the room and scrambled for an explanation. But Tom was less subtle.

"What did you do to her?" Tom was a big guy, so he had no problem jerking Eric to his feet.

"Tom!" I grabbed his arm, but it was no use.

"No," Jeanine cried, "he didn't do anything!"

Tom had Eric pinned to the wall as I leaned down to help Jeanine. She was cold and shaking, not unlike the way she had been last night. When I thought she had seen a ghost.

"Look, man." Eric put his hands in the air. "I didn't touch her, I swear."

"Tom!" I yelled. "Put him down. Now."

Tom took his hands off Eric and I breathed a sigh of relief. Jeanine stayed on the floor while I comforted her. Her eyes were on Eric, and I didn't know what to make of it.

"What happened?" I felt her face, and she was cold as ice.

"I don't know." She shook her head. "I don't know."

"Some guy came to the door," Eric volunteered. "I think she knows him."

"Who?" Tom crossed his arms over his chest and finally gave Eric some room to breathe. But that didn't stop him from crowding Jeanine. "Who was it?"

"Tom, give her some space. Why are you so angry?" I glared at him.

"We didn't let him in," Eric said. "But he left this."

Eric showed us two tickets to see the Atlanta Braves tomorrow afternoon. And if I wasn't mistaken, the seats were right beside ours. Or rather, the seats I had stolen from Ricky.

"Jeanine, who was at the door?" I asked. "Is that who you saw last night?"

She took a breath and nodded, while tears streamed down from her eyes.

"Well who was it?" Tom pressed, stepping closer. He needed to learn to be more patient.

"I don't know!" she finally said, breaking down into heaving sobs.

"And you're sure he didn't hurt you?" Tom pointed at Eric.

"What are you talking about?" Eric piped up. "I would never—"

"No." Jeanine dried her eyes. "Of course not."

Glaring at Tom, I helped Jeanine onto the bed and looked at the tickets.

"We're going to that game tomorrow." Tom touched my arm and left the room. When the door clicked shut, I glanced at Eric and knew he wasn't lying. Jeanine put her head on my shoulder and stared at the TV screen.

The *Titanic* was going belly up, and Leo was holding on for dear life.

Deep down, I wondered if we all should have been doing the same.

## Chapter 13

**E**ric never went home that night.

Once Jeanine calmed down, Tom took him to the store. They found jumper cables and tried to jump Eric's car off. But the problem wasn't with the battery.

So Eric spent the night in his parents' hotel room and agreed to go to the baseball game with us. While Jeanine and I got ready, I wondered what sort of trap we were walking into. I hadn't told her where I'd gotten the first two tickets. Nor had I taken the time to point out how odd it was that she and Eric had been given two more.

I couldn't wrap my head around it—the strange things happening in Atlanta. But maybe it was all just a coincidence. On the way to the game, I kept telling myself that.

It was the only way to keep the paranoia at bay.

In my seventeen years, I had never been to an

MLB game. Tom was more interested in football. And Jeanine—well, I think we all know the celebrity classified as her favorite sport.

But Eric was a baseball fan. And living in Atlanta had solidified his love for the Braves.

Getting to the stadium was a madhouse. Not at all different from the handful of college football games I'd been to. Pushing and shoving. Too many people. Not enough room.

When we reached our seats, I breathed a sigh of relief. We weren't too far from the field. But I was desperate to raid a concession stand for food and drinks.

"These are great seats!" Eric yelled over the crowd.

He sat on the other side of Jeanine, while I snuggled up to Tom. It was the first fun thing I'd done all summer—going to that baseball game. With my best friend on my left and the love of my life on my right, I couldn't think of a better way to spend the day.

Eric perked up. "The game's about to start."

I curled my arm around Tom and whined in his ear until he stood up. When he returned with lemonade and two hot dogs, I kissed him on the cheek. The sun was in my face and the wind was blowing the wrong way. But I didn't care. In fact, I felt free.

For two months, I had needed this. *We* had needed this. A break.

During the fourth inning, we were up by nine. I

put my head on Tom's shoulder and held his hand, feeling sleepy beneath the heavy sunshine. The Braves were playing the Phillies. And while I knew nothing about baseball, it was exciting.

Despite what had happened last night, Jeanine seemed happy. She kept leaning in to Eric, and I caught him whispering in her ear. He made her laugh, and I took that as a good sign.

But Tom sat there grunting like a sore sport. He kept giving Eric the evil eye, and I wanted to slap him upside the head. Would he get over it already? Eric wasn't the one freaking Jeanine out at night. It was someone else. Someone who wanted to talk.

In the middle of the fifth inning, I shielded my eyes from the sun. It felt too bright all of a sudden, and I kept blinking to stop it from blinding me.

"You okay?" Tom noticed my discomfort and put his hand on my shoulder.

"Yeah." I winced at the brightness. "I think I'm gonna go to the bathroom."

"Okay. Why don't you take Jeanine with you?"

I looked over at her with stars in her eyes. After a couple of trying nights, she deserved a sweet date with a good guy. And I didn't want to interrupt hers with Eric.

"I'll be fine." I stood up and Tom grabbed my hand. "Tom."

He turned his cheek and pointed to the center of it. Grinning from ear to ear, I leaned in and left a kiss there. Only then did he loosen his hold and release me.

"I'll be right back!" I shouted over the crowd.

By now, I should have learned not to make promises I couldn't keep.

After climbing the stairs, I wandered the stadium in search of the ladies' room. Delicious scents wafted over from the concession stand, as I made a mental note to stop there on the way back. Surely, Tom would appreciate a soft drink and some cotton candy.

Especially after the delicious lunch he'd purchased for me.

The line to the bathroom was ridiculously long. When I found it, my heart sank. The whole game would be over before I got a stall. So I kept going in search of a single bathroom. Even when a bright light kept shining in my face.

I shielded my eyes to block out the sun. But the blinding light felt more like reflective metal or glass. Eventually, I lucked out and found an empty restroom.

And the bothersome light simply went away.

I slipped into the restroom and found two stalls. It was so dark I could hardly see a thing. When I found the light switch it wouldn't work. But after downing a sixteen-ounce lemonade, I was desperate to relieve myself. So I wasn't really paying attention.

Once I finished, the main door creaked open. I heard the commentator over the sound system outside. And the lights flickered as the door swung shut.

My heart raced at the sound of heavy footsteps. I stepped on the toilet and squatted down to conceal my feet. If it looked like the place was empty, maybe they would leave.

I heard the faucet running and peeked through a crack in the door.

There was a man standing in front of the sinks.

Fear pulsed through my veins as I scooted back. The man lit a cigarette in front of the mirror. While I tried to make out his face, I lost my composure and the tank lid slammed into the wall. I put my hand over my mouth and closed my eyes, curling into the fetal position. I said every prayer you can think of. And some that don't even exist.

When I looked through the crack, he was gone. I waited for the door to shut, but there was nothing. So I held my breath and counted to ten, planning my escape.

But then he kicked the stall door in and grabbed me.

The minute I screamed, he threw me against the wall like a rag doll. I crumpled to the floor and touched the blood on my head. Then he was on top of me.

He ripped my shirt and put his hands around my neck. I pushed against his chest to fight him off, but it was no use. He was too strong. All heavy weight and bulging muscle.

For a second, I thought he was going to kill me. I couldn't breathe. And the burning in my chest was more than I could take. It felt like I was drowning.

When he stood up, I held on to his pant leg. I coughed and gasped for breath, moaning in agony. But he grabbed a baseball bat and held it over his head.

The door swung open and he dropped the bat.

Someone else was here.

I listened to the bat roll across the floor. Then there were footsteps.

I opened my mouth and cried out for help. But there were no words.

One of them hit me on the back of my head.

And then everything went black.

\* \* \*

They found me in the trunk of Tom's car the next day with a bag over my head. There was tape on my mouth and rope around my wrists. When Tom freed me, I crashed into him.

My ears were still ringing and everything hurt. Tom picked me up in his arms and carried me to a bedroom upstairs. It took me a while to adjust—to figure out where I was.

I'd never been to Eric's house before. Not the one in Atlanta. But from the looks of it, his parents were doing well for themselves.

I roused awake a few hours after they found me. I heard Eric and Jeanine out in the hall. They were trying to be quiet, I guess. But I wouldn't exactly call it whispering.

"What the hell happened?" Eric said.

"If you don't keep your voice down—"

"Screw keeping my voice down!" Eric shouted. "As long as you're all staying in *my* house, I want to know what the hell is going on!"

"Eric, please," Jeanine coaxed. "You don't know what we've all been through."

I heard footsteps and then a door slammed.

Then more footsteps.

Tom opened the door and slipped inside. While I would've climbed a mountain to get closer to him, I could barely move. So he came to me.

"Hey." He sat down on the side of the bed. "How are you feeling?"

"Everything hurts."

He put the back of his hand to my forehead, and I leaned into his touch. Then he trailed his fingers down my neck.

"Don't stop." I looked into his eyes, squeezing his hand.

He cupped my cheek. "I don't want to hurt you."

"You won't." I ran my hand down his arm.

Clearing his throat, Tom lay down on the bed facing me. Then he ran his thumb along my jawline. It felt so good, I whimpered.

"Are you ever gonna tell me what happened?" He placed his hand on my shoulder. "When you disappeared at the game, we called the cops. And then you weren't at the hotel. I was scared."

"You shouldn't have done that." I turned to lay

flat on my back.

"What? Called the cops?" He propped up on his elbow and tucked a lock of hair behind my ear.

I nodded.

Tom curled my body into his, running his fingers through my hair. "What happened to you, baby? What did they do to you?"

I could hear the tears in his voice. But I didn't want him to cry. I didn't have time to cry.

"Come on, Addie." He rubbed my arm. "You gotta tell me what happened."

I sat up against the headboard and winced the whole way there. "I'll tell you," I agreed. "Only you. But you have to promise me you'll never ask me to tell you again."

"Okay." Tom took my hand. "I promise."

"Nothing I say can leave this room."

Tom cocked his brow but eventually nodded.

"You remember when I went to the bathroom? At the baseball game?"

"Yes."

"They had a line out the door. But then I found one that was empty. So I went inside. It was dark—the lights didn't work."

Tom rubbed the back of my hand, coaxing the words out of me.

"Someone came in, so I hid in my stall. I saw a man through a crack in the door. He was standing in front of the mirrors."

My throat closed up on me before I could manage the rest. Tom rubbed my arms when he realized I was hyperventilating. I'm not sure if it was anxiety or a panic attack.

"Did they touch you?" he asked.

I stroked his cheek and whispered, "Yes."

## Chapter 14

I woke up in a dark room. There was laughter in the distance. The kind made by gentleman playing poker and smoking cigars. Only men like that were less frightening.

As I leaned up, the hard bed squeaked beneath me. Everything ached.

My mouth was dry.

My skin was cold.

Even my teeth hurt.

It wasn't until I was running my fingers through my hair that I realized...

I couldn't remember anything.

Where was I? Who were these people? What did they want from me?

Someone pushed the door open and I slid beneath the covers to hide. Despite the darkness, he saw me. And grabbed me. And bound me.

By the time he put the bag over my head, I was

crying.

He led me out of the room, kicking at my heels. And when they saw me, the laughter stopped.

I heard the squeak of a metal chair. Grating against the cement. And he pushed against my shoulder to sit me down. It was a hard seat. No cushion. No give.

When he tied my arms to the back of the chair, I didn't flinch.

Nor did I shudder when he kissed my neck.

I wasn't a newbie. I had done this before. The whole kidnapping thing.

I just hoped they couldn't see how fast my heart was beating.

Last time they had gone easy on me.

Last time had been a test.

What were the odds that I could live to tell the same tale twice?

What if this time, they killed me?

There were footsteps. Noises reminiscent of musical chairs. Without the music.

I sat there plotting a way to escape. Could I tear myself free from these ropes?

Without a knife?

He took the bag off my head and I gasped. I'm not sure why. It wasn't like I hadn't been able to breathe. But the way I inhaled—you would've thought I'd been drowning at sea.

There was a light bulb swinging over my head. And it blinded me for those first few seconds.

When I was brave enough to open my eyes, I tried to blink them away.

But there they were. All three of them sitting at a table in front of me.

I saw DeMilo first. Only because he was in the middle. He hadn't aged much. Then again, it had only been a couple of months since I saw him last. On a night I'd always remember.

Hugh slouched to his left, smoking a cigarette. He had always fascinated me. Because I couldn't understand how someone so beautiful could be so cruel, so callous, so mean.

And there was a third man. On the other side of DeMilo. I didn't recognize him.

But he looked like a criminal. Long stringy hair. An untrimmed beard. A few silver teeth. Tattoos covered his olive skin. Like someone had stamped every muscle.

"Are you gonna start or not?" DeMilo looked right through me.

That's when I realized someone was behind me. The man who had taken off the bag.

He ran his fingers down my neck. And my skin crawled with anticipation.

I heard his footsteps as he stepped into the light. So I could see him with my own eyes.

Somehow, I knew before I saw him. Maybe it was the memory of his touch. Like a branding iron on my skin. He had left me marked. And there was no erasing the scars.

Ricky was alive.

He caressed my face and traced the seam of my lips. Tears were rolling down my cheeks. Big fat ones. The kind I cried when he made me fall out of love with him.

I never loved Ricky. Not like Nicki did. But I *had* liked him.

It was more than a crush. More than flutters and butterflies in my stomach.

Ricky Travis was the first guy I ever dreamed about. Long before I met Tom.

He was just so tall and attractive. A football player. A jock. An athlete. A hottie.

Maybe that was why I loved Tom so much. Because he had all the good looks of his cousin. But he had a good heart, too. And for the men in their family, that was saying a lot.

"Happy to see me?" Ricky grabbed my face and planted his mouth on mine.

I pulled away and kicked him. Hard. He even fell down on the floor.

The older men laughed. And Hugh lit another cigarette.

"You shouldn't be here," I said. "You *can't* be here."

Ricky stood up and brushed himself off. There was malice in his eyes.

"Care to speed things up, son?" DeMilo drummed his fingers on the table.

I thought Ricky was going to hit me. I was prepared for it. He'd taught me to brace myself.

"Where is it?" Ricky stared into my eyes. His

were amber like whiskey.

I opened my mouth and took a breath. The men at the table were watching me.

So I played dumb. "What are you talking about?"

Wrong move.

He slapped me so hard I thought my ears might bleed. They were already ringing. But now my jaw was sore. So I put my head on my shoulder to rest. Then he grabbed my chin, and I had no choice but to look at him.

His breath was my breath. And in that moment, it was almost like we were one.

"I don't know," I shuddered. "But I don't have it. I swear to God."

Ricky smiled. I had learned to fear that smile a long time ago.

He reached into his pocket and began putting on rings. One for each finger.

"Wait." I caught my breath, biting the edge of my lip. "I'll tell you everything."

He left the rings on anyway. And when I looked at DeMilo, he nodded.

"After Daniel died, we found the necklace upstairs in his house. I don't know how it got there." I shut my eyes. "Tom wanted to bury it in the forest. So we did."

"Where?" Ricky crossed his arms. They looked bigger. Too big.

"A couple miles into the woods. We went back there to check. But it was gone."

"Lies." Hugh took a puff of smoke. "She's lying."

"I'm not lying!" I stared into syrupy eyes. "Ricky, I'm not lying."

He was calm at first. He even nodded to make me think he had accepted it.

But then he ripped the buttons on my shirt. One by one—they fell to the floor. With the exception of a pink floral bra, my torso was completely exposed. And I was ashamed.

Ricky snatched the elastic band out of my ponytail. And my hair tumbled down. Golden locks framed my face until he tucked them behind my ears. He was standing so close that I could taste his breath. He smelled like liquor and sweat.

"You have a pretty face." He pressed the tip of a blade to my lower lip. "That's why I don't believe you."

"You have a pretty face, too." I lifted my chin. "It's a shame you don't look that way on the inside."

"That's it." Ricky cut the rope on my wrists. "There are better ways to get the truth out of you."

As soon as my hands were free, I shot up and grabbed the chair. When it crashed down on him, I almost couldn't believe it. Ricky wiped the blood on his face and came after me with the knife. Try as I might, he pinned my arms to my chest.

And then the blade was at my throat.

"We started something," he whispered in my ear. "And we're going to finish it."

He dragged me out of there kicking and screaming. I turned to DeMilo and Hugh for mercy, even the stranger with stringy hair. But they weren't going to save me.

When I kicked him in the thigh, Ricky slammed my head against the wall. Then we were at the door, and he tossed me on the bed. The same room I'd just woken up in.

He didn't even bother to shut the door. I think that's what bothered me most.

When it came to my body, my feelings, my soul—he didn't care.

Doors were created for a reason. Privacy was desirable. Even for a rape victim.

He came towards me and pinned my arms over my head.

"NO!" This could not be happening again. I *would not* let this happen again.

"I'll bet he can't touch you like I can." His mouth was on my neck. "In fact, I'll bet you're still a virgin. You're not his anymore, Addie. You belong to me."

I stared at the ceiling and swallowed.

"You've *always* belonged to me."

While he unzipped his pants, I picked up a lamp and smashed it over his head.

"No, I don't!" I dragged him on the floor. The way he'd just dragged me.

Then I kicked him. And hit him. And climbed on top of him.

He struggled beneath me when I started

choking him. But I couldn't stop.

I *had* to kill him. I just had to.

When his legs were kicking, I squeezed harder. I was sucking the life out of him.

Hugh came in and pulled me away. That's the only reason I stopped.

"One day, someone is going to kill you," I said. "And I'm going to smile."

Ricky sat against the wall with heaving breaths, his hands around his neck.

So I didn't kill him. But man I wanted to. I never knew it felt like that. *Bloodlust.*

"I believe you know where the necklace is," DeMilo said.

They tied me up in the same chair. But they didn't touch me like Ricky had.

"And what makes you think that?" I hissed.

Almost killing Ricky boosted my confidence. I felt a sense of power. I wasn't afraid.

"Maybe you don't have it. But you know someone who does."

"What do you want me to do?" I struggled with the rope, and it burned my wrists.

"What I always want you to do." DeMilo stood up. "Find it."

He was walking away until I said, "And if I don't?"

"Then everyone you love will die."

I narrowed my eyes at the back of his head. "Including your grandson?"

"If he stands in my way, then yes."

"What is it about this necklace that's so *damn* special?" I spit on the ground.

"You could say it's a matter of life or death."

"Well, what do you want me to do about it?" I was beyond feeling like a captive.

"Why don't you ask that father of yours?" DeMilo put those hawk eyes on me.

"Jeffrey?" I snickered. "He doesn't know—"

"No," he interrupted. "Your *real* father. The man you saw at the institute. I believe he told you to call him *Jimmy.*"

I turned white as a ghost. "I don't have a father."

"Why don't you pay him a visit? Find out for yourself."

The nameless man hit me in the head.

Just before I blacked out, I saw Ricky coming to.

# Chapter 15

I didn't tell Tom that Ricky was alive. I honestly didn't think he'd believe me. Especially since I didn't understand it myself. No part of his presence made sense.

But maybe he was simply a magician who'd pulled off the greatest trick of all.

As far as Jimmy was concerned, I left that part out too. I hadn't planned on keeping so much from Tom. Look how much my life had suffered from being kept in the dark.

I guess there really wasn't much to tell. Because the story hadn't changed.

DeMilo wanted the necklace. And he was willing to kill everyone if I didn't get it.

But why me? Why was I always the one responsible for hunting the necklace down? And then he expected me to deliver it to him like someone who worked at the post office.

If he knew where the necklace was, why couldn't he get it himself?

DeMilo claimed to know the secrets I held dear. But none of them involved the necklace. I was just as mystified as him. We had buried the necklace in the earth.

But it was gone now. Surely, he knew I was telling the truth. After all, wasn't it his men running through the wilderness at night? Leaving bloody notes on my doorstep?

The main question—if neither of us had the necklace, then where was it?

I had every intention of finding out. So I snuck outside on the pretense of getting some fresh air. Before I walked out the door, Tom hugged me like he wasn't going to let go.

I put my head on his chest and took his keys like a pick pocket on the street. They were in his back pocket, and I hoped he didn't notice they were missing. When I drove away, tears were streaking down my face. Maybe because of the physical pain. I hurt all over.

At the Art Institute, I headed upstairs and stared at that painting in the hall. The one I wanted to buy. The one he wouldn't sell. The one that reminded me of Daniel.

Yesterday had given me confidence. Because I had no problem walking in during Jimmy's class. He stepped outside the classroom to talk to me. And I watched everything he did. When he put his hand on my shoulder, I accepted his invitation to sit in.

So I took a seat in the back and paid attention. Jimmy was a gifted sketch artist. He replicated a woman's face in twenty minutes. And the class applauded him at the feat.

But I collected my things and walked out. Was it true? Could Jimmy really be my father?

While the class let out, I waited for him in the hall. The paintings captured my attention. I looked for a signature at the bottom. Something to credit the artist.

"Addie." He stood beside me. "Why don't we talk in my office?"

"Who is the artist?" I looked at the artwork on the wall. "Where is the signature?"

Jimmy looked down.

"Do you know what's happening here?" I asked. "I'm tired of playing games."

He furrowed his brow. "What are you talking about?"

"You sent my acceptance letter in the mail. It wasn't an accident."

He crossed his arms and leaned against the wall. "Yes."

"Why?" I stared him in the eye. "Why do you want me here?"

Jimmy cupped my cheek in his hand. Then he looked closer, noticing the bruises. I'd done my best to cover them up. But there were so many, I'd run out of concealer.

"Addie." He brushed the hair off my neck and

spotted an unsightly gash.

"I'm not the best with makeup."

He put his arm around me. For the first time, I wanted DeMilo to be right. I wanted a father. A *real* father. One who wanted me. Just as much as I wanted him.

In the teacher's lounge, he grabbed a pack of ice and some water. He put the ice on my bruises as I sipped on the water. But everything was so cold. In no time, I was shivering.

Jimmy tossed a blanket over my shoulders, and we sat in the lounge for hours talking. I asked him what he was like as a child, where he had grown up. Savannah was his home. But he hadn't been back in years. Both of his parents were dead. He was an only child.

"So how come you never got married? Never had children?"

Jimmy eased the tension in the back of his neck. Then he rested his elbows on his knees, staring down. His eyes stayed on the floor for minutes. Until he spoke again.

"I loved one woman. But she left me."

"Why?" I put my water down and curled up under the blanket.

He folded his hands. "I don't know."

My hands were shaking. I felt like throwing up. But I had to ask. I had to know.

"Are you my father?"

Apathy was written all over his face. "Sorry kid. I can't be your dad."

"You're lying!" I wanted him to be so badly.

"I knew your grandfather. He sent me copies of your work. That's how you got in."

"Daniel?" I would play dumb if I had to. If it was the only way to get it out of him.

"Whose paintings do you think are hanging up on that wall out there?"

"If those are Daniel's paintings, then why do you have them?" I asked.

"He donated them to the institute." Jimmy nursed a hot cup of coffee.

"Where were you when he died?" I huffed. "If the two of you were so close?"

"I heard about his death." He put his hand on my knee. "And I'm very sorry for your loss."

I stood up and paced the floor, holding the blanket around me. "You saw the bruises on my neck. You know what's going on. So why are you pretending like you don't?"

He looked at his watch. "It's getting late. Why don't we talk in my office?"

"Okay." I had left a note for Tom, hoping that was enough to keep him at bay.

As Jimmy led me down the hall, I wondered if DeMilo was lying. When you were least expecting it, he had a funny way of telling the truth. That's why I believed him.

It was dark outside. Everyone must have left the building but us. I wondered if it was safe to be alone with him. A man I wanted to believe was my true father.

Jimmy unlocked the door to his office, and I stepped inside. Apart from the glow of a computer screen, we were in complete darkness. But then he turned on the lights.

And I saw Antoinette's portrait hanging on the wall.

A million possibilities flashed before my eyes.

Was he in on it?

Was he one of them?

Had I walked into a trap?

"It was you." I spun around as he locked the door. "You broke into the mansion. You stole the portrait. You—"

"Returned the necklace? Yes. And it was safe. Until you moved it."

"Where is it?" I pulled a knife out of my pocket. "Show me!"

He held his hands in the air. "Addie, you don't know who you're dealing with."

"I'm out of patience, Mr. Blake. Show it to me! Now!"

I put the blade against his throat and forced him in front of the painting.

"You've put me in an awkward position, Addie." He took the painting off the wall. And there was a hidden safe behind it. Somehow, I wasn't even surprised.

"Open it." I gritted my teeth, breaking out in a cold sweat.

"If I give it to you, you'll never be safe again."

"Just do it!" I was beyond kindness and

subtlety. "Do it!"

So Jimmy gave in and spun the dial on the lock. When it clicked open, I saw the necklace with my own eyes. It was resting on a velvet display. Polished and sparkling.

"You had it cleaned," I noted.

"Yes." He unhooked the clasp and put the necklace on me.

It felt heavier than normal. I touched the stone. And everything felt right.

"What's so special about it?" I asked. "My grandmother's necklace?"

"I'll tell you some time." He tucked the pendant beneath my shirt. "But for now, keep it safe. Don't bury it in the ground. Throw it in the ocean. Put it in a place even you'll forget."

"How is that keeping it safe?"

"Because no one will come looking for it. And that will keep *you* safe." He lifted my chin. "But you have to promise me that one day, you'll destroy it."

"Destroy it? Why on earth would I do that?"

"Because you don't want it getting into the wrong hands."

"I don't understand." I shook my head. Nothing made sense anymore.

He threaded his fingers through my hair and kissed my forehead.

"It might destroy life as we know it."

There was banging on the door. I heard Ricky yelling on the other side.

"Go!" I pulled Jimmy's arm. "Through the window. Before they see you."

Jimmy stopped at the window and looked back.

"If they know you've had it all this time, they'll kill you."

Ricky kicked the door in and grabbed me. I fought against him as he set the man with stringy hair on Jimmy. Hugh stepped into the room and put on a pair of brass knuckles.

"No!" I reached out for him. But Ricky hit me so hard I blacked out.

When I woke up, we were in the back seat of a moving car. Ricky broke the chain around my throat. And I watched him hand the necklace to someone in the front seat.

Hugh sealed the necklace in a velvet box, while I felt the marks on my neck.

"Good work, beautiful." Ricky opened my door and pushed me out.

I tumbled across the pavement and heard tires screeching in the distance. Then I lay on the ground at the side of the road. My body was covered in fresh bruises. There was blood in my hair. But I actually felt relieved. For the first time in my life, they were gone.

They were *truly* gone.

Maybe Jimmy was right. When it came to the necklace, my safest choice was to get rid of it. Now DeMilo had the necklace, and they had no reason to come knocking on my door.

After lying there for an hour, I had yet to see a single car come by. So I got up and walked until the city came into view. Then I took a taxi to the Art Institute.

When I arrived, Jimmy was leaving. I jumped out of the taxi and ran over to him. He had a black eye and there were bruises on his face. But at least he was alive.

"Jimmy, I'm so sorry. I didn't want them to hurt you."

He wiped dust off my face. "You should go home. Get out of Atlanta."

"What about you?" I leaned into his chest. "What if they come back?"

"They have what they want. They won't be coming back anytime soon."

We walked to his car as my taxi pulled away. So Jimmy offered to give me a ride. Our last chance to catch up before I returned to Savannah. And never saw him again.

"So tell me about your boyfriend," he said. "Are you going to marry him?"

"Jimmy." I watched the road. "I'm only seventeen."

"I was seventeen when I fell in love. And I would have married her."

I bit my tongue and looked out the window. "What did she look like?"

"Blonde hair. Pretty face." He turned at a red light. "Green eyes—like yours."

I stared at him until he looked at me. "What

happened to her?"

"I'm not really sure. She disappeared out of my life. I never heard from her again."

We were quiet until Jimmy pulled into the driveway. Tom was standing in front of Eric's house. And he looked pissed. I cracked my knuckles and swallowed.

"Looks like you've got some explaining to do," Jimmy said.

"What do I tell him?" I unfastened my seatbelt. "If he knows too much, it might hurt him."

"I don't know." He shifted the car into park. "That's for you to decide."

"Thanks for the ride." I gave him a hug and whispered in his ear, "Dad."

He let me go. My heart broke all over again when I watched him drive away.

"Where the hell have you been?" Tom grabbed my arm. "You steal my car. You don't answer your phone. You won't cooperate with the police. I've been worried sick! Do you know—"

"Okay!" I put some distance between us. "I get it."

"If it hadn't been for Jimmy, I wouldn't even know what happened."

"What?" I shielded my eyes from the sunlight.

"He called me last night. And you're lucky I didn't—"

"They have the necklace now. It's over. They're gone."

Tom did a double take. "What?"

"Jimmy knew Daniel. He had the necklace. He was keeping it safe."

Tom took a step closer. He had that look on his face like he didn't believe me.

"But now DeMilo has it. So it's over. They have what they want."

"You just let him take it?" Tom said. "Just like that?"

"I think our lives are more important than some stupid necklace."

As my words sank in, Tom believed me. "Come here, baby."

I leaned in and wrapped my arms around him. He held me closer.

"I was so worried about you." He kissed me on the mouth, the cheek, the forehead.

"It's okay." I put my hands on his chest. "I've taken care of it. We're safe now."

He touched a tender spot and I flinched. "Let's get you cleaned up."

"Wait." I burrowed my face in the crook of his neck. "I'm sorry I left."

"It's okay." He rubbed my shoulders and back. "Where is my car?"

"Sorry, I forgot about it. I guess it's still at the institute."

He nodded with a smile. "Don't worry. I'll go back and get it."

Wrapping my arms around him, I took a breath in, absorbing his warmth.

"Are you ready to go home?" he asked.

"Yes."

## Chapter 16

Words can't describe the way Eric looked at me. Like he didn't know who I was. Jeanine welcomed me with open arms. And I'm sure she wasn't surprised by the bruises.

But Eric couldn't cope. He wanted to know everything. He wanted to call the cops.

All pointless attempts at seeking justice. He had been away from Savannah for far too long. And we'd only brought the dangers of the forest here. To his safe haven in Atlanta.

After I took a warm shower, Tom bandaged me up. Despite the abuse, I felt so relieved. It wasn't like the time before. Now, I knew our dealings with DeMilo were finally over. I wasn't afraid because I'd made the ultimate bargain with him.

The necklace for a long, happy life.

I had things to look forward to. A future with

Tom. It was a decision I'd never regret.

"You're leaving?" Eric saw us packing. "What *the hell* happened?"

"I got into trouble with the wrong people," I said. "But it's over now."

He ruffled his blonde locks. "So you're just gonna leave? What about the institute?"

"I never applied." I zipped my suitcase. "It was just a big misunderstanding."

Tom grabbed our bags and left to pack the car. Eric and I were alone in the room.

"But we'll still see you in Savannah. Right?" I slapped him on the shoulder.

"Yeah." He led me out the door looking lost. "I guess so."

"We can hang out all the time." I hugged. "It will be great. Just like old times."

Eric saw Jeanine standing in the hallway. They looked sad to say goodbye.

So I left them alone and waited for her in the car. When she got in the back seat, Tom pulled out of the drive. Eric stood there waving at us. And Jeanine looked back.

"It's not like you're never going to see him again," I reassured her.

"I know," she pouted. "But we were just getting to know each other."

I looked at her in the rearview mirror. "You're fifteen. You've got plenty of time."

Even though we were all tired, it was a fun trip home. Tom stopped by a couple drive-thrus and ordered our favorite treats. For Jeanine, it was like a consolation prize.

Her relationship with Eric would develop over time. I knew she couldn't see that now, because DeMilo had clouded her judgment. No wonder she was feeling *carpe diem.*

Since murder and mayhem had entered my life, I'd turned to it as well.

After we took Jeanine home, Tom and I headed for the outskirts of town. When I walked in the front door, he said something about dinner. And I loved how *normal* that sounded. Just a nice quiet evening at home with the love of my life.

"Addison Smith!"

Or not.

Eleanor pinched my arm until I squealed. "What? Get off me!"

"I give you condoms and you run off to Atlanta?" She was furious.

"Condoms?" Jeffrey walked into the room. "Who said anything about condoms?"

"Maybe I should get going." Tom squeezed my hand, headed for the door.

"Yeah," Jeffrey said. "I was just about to—"

"Sit down and shut up!" Eleanor pointed at the sofa. It took some groveling, but eventually I sat down. Jeffrey plopped down to my right, while Tom settled on the left.

Tom held my hand. As our fingers laced together, I knew a time would come when I didn't need them anymore. My so-called parents. I needed Tom more.

"Now." Eleanor stood tall. "When did it become okay for you to skip town without asking *my* permission first?"

"Well, you leave without asking mine, so—"

"What was that?" Her eyes looked black. "Up to your room now! You're grounded!"

"You can't ground me!" I tried to stand, but Tom held me back.

"Yeah, Eleanor, I think you're being too hard on her."

Tom and I looked at Jeffrey in shock. So he speaks. About time.

"Excuse me?" She glared at him.

"I think I'll just let you handle this."

"No." She blocked his escape. "You'll stay right here."

Jeffrey ducked his head. Well, that was short-lived.

"Now I understand it's summer, but I've had enough of this, Addison!" she screamed. "You're not allowed to see each other anymore. Is that understood?"

I almost laughed in her face. "You can't keep me away from Tom."

"What did you say to me?"

I stood up and got in her face. "I'll be eighteen in four months. And he lives in my grandfather's house. The one I'm going to inherit. Don't tell me I can't see him again."

Eleanor looked confused, at a loss for words.

Like she couldn't believe I was standing up to her.

"I saw your bags by the door," I said. "I guess that means you're leaving again."

"Tomorrow."

"Jeffrey!" Eleanor shot him a nasty look.

"What?" He stood up and took my side. "She's right."

"You're not my mother. I don't have to do what you tell me to."

That rendered her speechless. If I'm not mistaken, Eleanor actually looked like she was about to cry. It tugged at my heartstrings, but I had to be strong. So I stayed firm with her.

"All right. Then we'll treat you like an adult now. If that's what you want."

"Thank you." I headed for the front door. "I'm staying with Tom tonight."

"You are?" Jeffrey looked disappointed. "Well, be careful."

Tom opened the door, and I left without looking back.

"Are you sure that's how you want to leave things with them?" he asked. "Before they go out of town? You don't know when they'll be back."

"I don't care." I got in his car and slammed the door. "Take me home."

Tom smiled once he realized I was talking about his place.

We spent the night planning out our future. Where we would go to college. When we would get married. How many kids. I couldn't believe he was comfortable with it.

Marriage talk. Not to mention, having children.

But Tom was just that kind of guy. He was a man—far too mature for boys the likes of his age. I crawled into his bed after he fell asleep and covered him with the sheet.

We lay like that until the sun came up the next morning. He looked like an angel.

\* \* \*

Maybe I'd been too tired to have a nightmare. But Ricky hadn't escaped my mind. Now that we were back, I knew I had to tell someone. For fear of going completely insane.

Tom would freak out. And Daniel wasn't here. So that left Jeanine.

After all that driving, Tom slept in late the next day. I made lunch plans with Jeanine, but he didn't want to come along. Atlanta had totally exhausted him. In a way, I was glad. Not because Tom was tired. But because it gave me a chance to talk to Jeanine. Alone.

We ordered appetizers for lunch. Onion rings. Loaded potato skins. Cheese sticks.

And I know that sounds unhealthy. But after the previous day, I needed carbs. Deep down, I had a feeling Jeanine was craving comfort food, too.

"Eric called last night." She took a sip of diet soda.

"Oh really?" I spread a napkin in my lap.

"Missing you already?"

She blushed. "He asked me out."

"Told you he likes you."

"Well, it won't be until he gets to Savannah," she said.

"But it's still a date. I'm happy for you. I think y'all will be good together."

She nodded, crumpling up the paper sleeve from her straw.

When our food came, I filled my plate with every fried delicacy. There was sour cream on the potatoes. And marinara sauce with the cheese sticks. Dipping sauces like ranch and honey mustard for the onion rings.

"Addie." Jeanine looked around the restaurant. "I need to tell you something."

I swallowed my first bite of potato. "All right. Let's hear it."

"Do you remember when I kept freaking out at the hotel? In Atlanta?"

"Yeah."

"I saw him." She lowered her voice and leaned in. "I saw Ricky."

I dropped my fork. We were eating finger food. But the fried cheese was way too hot to touch. Especially when it had just come out of the oven. I dropped my knife, too.

"I know how it sounds," she said. "But I'm not crazy. I swear it was—"

"I saw him, too."

"Then you know—you know he's still alive."

"Yes."

"What are we going to do? He's my brother, but he scares me."

I took a sip of water. "What was Nicki doing at your house the other day?"

"What?" She tilted her head to the side.

"When I came over, she darted out the front door. You didn't know she was there?"

"No." Her lips curved down at the edges. "I didn't let her in."

"She must have a key."

"Who would give her a key?"

I gave her a look, because the answer was so obvious.

"Oh. My brother."

"Jeanine, why didn't you tell me it was Ricky? I thought you were seeing a ghost."

"So did I." She took a bite out of an onion ring. "Believe me."

I looked over the food on my plate, picking at the stringy cheese. It was mozzarella—my favorite. But after gorging myself, the thought of Ricky turned my stomach upside down.

"Why didn't you tell me?" Jeanine asked. "After everything that happened."

"I don't know." I licked a drop of marinara. "I didn't think anyone would believe me."

Jeanine nodded as the waiter took our plates away. Originally, dessert had been on the agenda. But now that we were on the same page, my appetite had left the room.

"I haven't told Tom." I unzipped my purse to pay the check.

"I don't know what to do about Mom and Dad." She looked down. "Ricky said he was going away for a while. I'm so happy he's alive. He's my brother. I love him."

How could I blame her for that?

"I understand. But he's not a good person. Even if he is your brother."

"Why is he always getting himself into trouble? I hate him for that."

"Me too." I left a tip. "I bet there is someone else who knows he's alive."

She thought about it. And then reality struck her right in the face. "Nicki."

"Why don't we pay her a visit?"

# Chapter 17

I'd never been to Nicki's house before. Trust me, I'd never had the desire to step foot in that place. But now I had an explanation for why she'd been acting so strange. On that last day of school, I thought it was a sign of mourning. The weight loss, the marks on her wrist.

But I was wrong. Nicki wasn't coping with Ricky's death. She was accepting his survival.

Jeanine and I talked about it on the ride over. How had Ricky escaped?

There was a coffin. But I never saw the body lying inside of it. Closed casket and all.

Jeanine mentioned a private viewing for the family. According to her, Ricky looked unrecognizable. I remembered the idle gossip on that cloudy day. His body was too marred for display. So no one was allowed to see his corpse. Or so I'd been told.

When we reached Nicki's house, I was surprised. At school, she always had the flashiest things. I would have thought Caldwell had them living in a mansion for sure.

"Is this the right place?" I put the car in park and looked out the windshield.

"That's it all right. It doesn't look like anyone's home."

Rain came down in sheets as I pulled the car into the driveway. "Great."

"Do you think we should have called first?" Jeanine grabbed her cell phone.

"I don't see the point now." I turned the car off. "We're already here."

"Well." She unbuckled her seat belt. "What are you going to say?"

"Something will come to me." I unlocked the doors and we made a run for it. The blinds were drawn, and it didn't look like anyone was in the house. So I ducked under the covering and rang the doorbell anyway. Then Jeanine got brave and knocked.

Since it was summer, I assumed Caldwell would answer the door. He was the last person I wanted to see, but I had to talk to Nicki. To my relief, she came to the door instead.

"What are you doing here?" She was wearing a loose jacket. And as she looked from me to Jeanine, she pulled it tightly around her. Like a shield. What was she guarding?

"Look, I know things have been weird between

us. I just wanted to talk to you."

"Sorry." She stepped back and went to shut the door. "Not interested."

"Wait." Jeanine put her hand on the door. "We know Ricky is alive."

Nicki tightened her jaw. She was awfully thin. I could see the bones in her cheeks.

"You're going to tell us everything you know about my brother." Jeanine stepped into the doorway and stared up at Nicki. "We're not leaving until you do."

"Fine." She rolled her eyes. "Come in."

I followed Jeanine into the foyer, and Nicki shut the door behind us. The living room was simple. A few couches and a recliner. I didn't even see a TV anywhere. But then I saw a portrait above the mantle. Her late mother, photographed in a professional studio.

She was gorgeous. Tall. Blonde. Thin. Like a supermodel.

And Nicki looked just like her.

"My room is upstairs." Nicki grabbed a bottle of Evian while I looked over my shoulder. Something about this house felt off. Like someone was watching us.

In her bedroom, Nicki collapsed on a twin size bed. There was a t-shirt on the pillow. Plastered with Georgia's football schedule. It must have belonged to Ricky.

"When is the last time you saw him?" Jeanine asked.

"Three weeks ago maybe. He came to my room at night. It was raining." She took a swig of Evian and looked out the window. I'm guessing that's how Ricky snuck in.

"When did you find out he was still alive?" I sat down by the window.

"That same night." She picked at the bottle wrapper. "He was weird."

"Weird how?" Jeanine took a seat on the floor. It was just the three of us talking.

"I don't know. He seemed different. He talked about you."

Nicki looked right through me. I knew she hated me. She always had.

"Me?" I poked my chest.

"Yeah." Nicki leaned against the wall behind her bed. "You."

"What did he say about me?"

"I don't know," she whined. "It wasn't really about you. It was more about that stupid necklace."

"What did he say about it?" Jeanine pressed.

"I don't know." She crawled under the covers. "He needs it. Soon."

"Soon. What—what does that mean?"

"If his grandfather doesn't have the necklace, someone will die."

I looked at Jeanine and she swallowed. DeMilo wasn't playing around.

"When are you seeing him again?" I said.

"I don't know," she repeated. "He doesn't

exactly call ahead."

"How have you been?" I took a chance and sat down on the bed. Her wrists were covered, but that's the first place my eyes went. "Are you still cutting yourself?"

Her eyes widened. "No."

"Whatever you're doing to yourself, stop it." I touched her shoulder. "He isn't worth it. No guy is worth your life. I don't care how good looking he is."

She shoved my hand away. "You would say that, wouldn't you?"

"What is that supposed to mean?"

"You have Tom. And he's gorgeous and rich and perfect."

I shook my head. "Tom is *not* perfect."

"Then why don't we talk about your boyfriend instead of criticizing mine."

"You're stomach." I tilted my head to get a better look at her midsection. "Why do you keep holding it like that?" Her hand had been there the whole time. "Does it hurt?"

Nicki opened a drawer and popped a couple pills. "So what if it does? Why do you care?"

"I want to know what happened to you." I grabbed her wrist. "I want to know you're okay."

"Why?" Nicki shuddered as mascara streaked down her face. She was crying.

"Because we've all been through hell. And I'm tired of all of us trying to face it alone."

Jeanine pulled her knees into her chest and

looked away.

"It's stupid!" I flinched when thunder rattled the walls.

The girls laughed, and it was the first time I really thought about it. What if things were different between us? Instead of hating each other, what if we could actually be friends?

Nicki dried her eyes and sat up in bed. When she was brave enough, I waited for her to tell me more. She showed me instead, rolling up the sleeves on her jacket.

I didn't say anything. Because it wasn't my place. I didn't want to judge her anymore.

"I've been taking anxiety pills. Sleeping pills. Some alcohol." Nicki shoved her fingers in her hair. "But I can't get him out of me." She squeezed her eyes shut.

I was going to say something, but Jeanine shook her head.

"It's like he's still here." She picked a hole in the bedding. "He won't leave me alone."

"Are you talking about—"

"The baby!" she screamed.

My mouth was gaping open. I turned to Jeanine. Neither of us knew what to say.

"I was pregnant. I found out in January. And Ricky was furious."

Nicki grabbed a couple tissues to dry her eyes.

"He said it was all my fault. I should have been more careful. He even wrote that stupid thing on my locker. Just to get back at me."

"Then why did you act like I did it? If you knew it was Ricky?" I asked.

"Because he told me to." She squeezed my hand. "Don't you get it? He's not like most guys. There's something about him. I thought it was sexy at first. But it scares me."

"It scares me too," Jeanine said.

"What happened to the baby?" I said.

"I lost it." She held her head between her knees.

Maybe I wasn't a doctor. But in my time around Eleanor, I'd picked up a thing or two.

"Naturally?"

"No," she moaned. "He made me get rid of it. He got rid of it."

"Nicki." I shook her arm. "Why didn't you go to the doctor? My mom? She would have helped you. She would have given you options."

"You. Don't. Understand." She rubbed her temples. "Ricky is like a god."

Jeanine covered her ears. "If this is about sex, I don't want to hear it!"

"It's not just the sex." She ran her fingers through her hair. "After being with him, I don't know how any other guy could ever measure up. I *want* to be with him."

"How can you want to be with someone that treats you like that?" I asked.

"I know it's messed up. But no matter what he does, I still love him."

Jeanine looked mystified.

"I don't know if it will always be like that," Nicki said. "But that's how it is now."

"You know Ricky isn't the monogamous type?" I said.

"I know." She nodded. "And I can accept that."

"How?" It didn't make any sense. "If Tom cheated on me, I would—"

"You say that," Nicki interrupted. "But would you? Would you really?"

Why would my mind go there? Tom wasn't the cheater. Ricky was.

"It's not as bad with you." She rubbed her knee. "I *know* you. But that other girl he sees. Well, I can't stand it." Her voice was laced with bitterness.

"What other girl?"

Was she talking about Jane? The girl I'd seen him kissing at the last house party? When I rescued Jeanine the next day? The volleyball player?

"You know her." Nicki despised the girl. "You were friends with her."

When I looked at her like she was crazy, Nicki went on.

"Blonde. Pretty. She kind of looks like you. Except her eyes aren't green. I think they're brown." She stared at the ceiling. "Or blue maybe. She has a brother. He's younger than us. What's his name?"

"Eric," I answered.

"Yeah." Nicki snapped her fingers. "That's him!"

"Oh my god." My heart skipped a beat. "Oh my god."

"What?" Nicki sat back. "What is it? What's wrong with you?"

"You're telling me Emily is still alive? She's been alive this whole time?"

"Yeah," she shrugged. "He keeps her in the woods. He sees her at night."

I rose from the bed and lost my breath. My head was spinning. I couldn't see straight.

"And you've known about this?" I asked. "For over a year?"

"It's not like I kidnapped her."

I charged and dragged her out of the bed. Then I slapped her until Jeanine dragged me away. Nicki fought back, but I managed to get a few more blows in. Until Jeanine came between us.

"For a second, I thought you might actually be a decent person," I snapped. "But I guess I was wrong."

"Come on, Addie." Jeanine pulled my arm. "Let's go."

"You're never going to find her."

I turned back in front of the door.

"Even I don't know where she is. Ricky only trusts himself."

"I'm glad your child died."

It was a low blow. Below the belt for sure. But

I had to make it.

"He deserves a better mother than you."

That's when Nicki started throwing things at us. We ran down the stairs and got the hell out of there. Caldwell was pulling into the neighborhood just as we escaped. If I hadn't been driving, I might have ducked down so he wouldn't see me.

But I kept on driving and looked him right in the eye. He saw me, and I knew all the deep, dark secrets his daughter had been keeping. I wondered how much he knew.

"Oh my god." Jeanine leaned her head against the window. "It's worse than I thought."

I kept my eyes on the road and sped up. "I hope you brought a rain coat."

"Why?"

"Because we're going into the woods."

## Chapter 18

**E**mily. My first real friend. We played together as children. She taught me how to paint my nails and braid my hair. How to do my own makeup. All the things Eleanor wouldn't.

I'd given up the hope long ago—that she might still be out there.

But Eric had been the last one to give up the ghost. I remember when his parents told him they were leaving, relocating to Atlanta. He was furious. And his last day in Savannah, I stayed up all night with him.

He couldn't stop crying. And it was painful to say goodbye, like ripping me in two.

Because when Eric left, it was with the memory of Emily. A sister more than a friend.

"Should we call the police?" Jeanine held on for dear life. "What do we do?"

"No." I turned on the windshield wipers.

"Nicki could be lying."

"You think she is?" Jeanine dropped her phone on the floorboard.

"No," I repeated. "I have a very good feeling she's telling the truth."

While I would have liked to look for Emily myself, that wasn't smart. There were many times when impatience had gotten me in the wrong situation. So I drove all the way home in silence, plotting my next move—a plan to find Emily in the forest. Alive.

"Addie." Jeanine pointed at the car in the drive.

"What is he doing here?" I parked in the garage and we headed inside.

This was bad timing. All of it was. He shouldn't be here.

"Hey!" Tom was making dinner in the kitchen. He wrapped his arm around me and planted a kiss on my cheek. "I wasn't sure when you'd be home."

"Tom, I have to tell you something."

Eric walked in the room. And he looked so happy to see us. Especially Jeanine.

How could we tell him? It was going to be hard enough telling Tom. He would be angry that I'd concealed Ricky from him. But now that we knew Emily was alive...

"Hey." There was hardly any breath in my words.

"Sorry to just drop by." Eric gave me a hug and

then turned to Jeanine.

"No it's fine." I grabbed Tom's arm and pulled him away. "Make yourself at home."

"What is it?" Tom whispered.

"What are you doing here?" Jeanine welcomed Eric's warm embrace.

But there was worry in her voice. The same anxiety creeping through my veins.

How were we going to tell him?

"My parents already bought the house. Just thought I'd get a head start on the moving process." Eric curled his arm around her small body. "Are you happy to see me?"

"Yes." She looked away. "It's just that... umm—"

"Jeanine, can I talk to you for a minute?" I let go of Tom and walked into the foyer. "Outside."

"Yeah." She left Eric and passed Tom in the kitchen.

I stood by the front door and handed her a rain coat. Then I put one on and pulled the hood over my head. Tom put his hands on his hips, clearly perturbed. But Eric just stared.

I walked out the door and closed it behind me. Jeanine was waiting on the front porch. So I gave her a look and stepped into the rain. "Let's go for a walk."

It was pouring, so we didn't have to go far. I didn't want to risk Eric or Tom hearing us. I had to think of a way to break the news to them first.

For Tom, Ricky would be his sole source of

agony. And he would hate me for lying to him about it. Well, lying by omission I guess. All I'd really done was leave it out.

But with Eric, the news would be a double whammy. Not only was Emily still alive. So was her captor. Eric had spent years begging for more time. Search parties. Police.

Sadly, nothing ever materialized. Eric liked being right, but not about this. If he knew Ricky was alive, he would kill him with his bare hands. And then end up in prison.

"What are we going to do?" Jeanine stood with her legs straight, biting her nails.

"I don't know." I was pacing between the trees. I didn't even mind the rain. "I wasn't expecting Eric to just show up like this. I need to think."

"Okay." She nodded and gave me space.

But the rain continued to pour. Before long, she was shivering.

"We could tell them at the same time," she suggested. "Two birds. One stone."

I turned my back to her and stared into the woods. "Tom will be a little pissed. But it's nothing like Eric. You don't know him like I do. When he finds out—"

"When I find out what?"

Jeanine gasped as I looked over my shoulder. Tom and Eric were standing behind us. We hadn't heard them walk up because of the rain.

"Addie," Tom smoldered. "What's going on?"

"Yeah." Eric took a step closer. "What are you

girls up to?"

Jeanine stood beside me, while I thought of the best way to tell them. Maybe there was no *right* way. Maybe quicker was better. Certainly not painless. Like a Band-Aid.

But when it was over, it was over.

"Ricky's alive." Jeanine broke into tears. "That's who I kept seeing in Atlanta."

Tom stared right through me. "What?"

"He's also one of the men who took me," I said.

"What?" Eric scratched his head. "Who is Ricky?"

"He's my brother." Jeanine sobbed as Eric moved in to comfort her.

"He's also the man who took your sister." I stopped Eric in his tracks. "Emily is still alive. She has been this whole time. And Ricky's been keeping her here. In the woods."

Eric looked at me and then turned to Jeanine.

"Hey, she didn't know." I wrapped my arm around her.

"What about you?" He narrowed his eyes. "How long have you known?"

The thunder moved closer. And I raised my voice so he could hear me.

"Eric, I just found out! But she's alive! And now we can find her!"

He backed away with shaky hands. Then he ran his fingers through his hair.

When he took off, Jeanine went after him.

"Eric wait!"

I was shivering. But when I turned to Tom for comfort, he was unresponsive.

"You lied to me." Drops of water skirted down his face. His hair was dripping wet.

"Tom, I wanted to tell you as soon as I found out but—"

"You didn't," he interrupted. "But you didn't."

He left me standing there in the rain. And I thought it was all stupid. Emily was out there. We should have been looking for her. There wasn't a moment to waste.

When I made it back to the house, Tom and Eric were on their way out. Jeanine was on the sofa crying. From the looks of it, little to nothing had been accomplished.

"Where are you going?" I squeezed Tom's arm in the doorway.

"To find my sister," Eric said. Then he got in his car and drove away.

"Tom." I held him back. "I want to come, too. Let me help you find her."

"No." He wouldn't even look at me. "It's too dangerous."

"Tom, I wanted to tell you. I promise!"

"If you wanted to, you would have. So why didn't you?"

"Tom." I burrowed my head in his chest. "Please don't leave like this."

But he withdrew and got in his car, driving off in the same direction as Eric. I walked inside and slammed the door. Jeanine flinched, huddling beneath a blanket on the couch.

"Well." I took off my rain coat and sat down beside her. "Now they know."

"Yeah."

I sat back and stared at the wall. "This is stupid."

"What is?" She grabbed a tissue and blew her nose.

"We're the ones who found out about Emily being alive." I got up to look out the window. "Why are we not allowed to be out looking for her?"

"I guess Tom and Eric are just trying to keep us safe."

"Emily was like a sister to me." I searched for my car keys. "I know her better than anyone else. And Ricky is your brother. You know him better than anyone else."

"Where are you going?" Jeanine sniffled.

"If anyone is going to find her, it's going to be us." I opened the front door. "Are you coming or not?"

Jeanine smiled and leapt to her feet. And we hurried out in the rain. Once we got in the car, I pulled out a map of Savannah. Ricky was clever, but so was Emily.

I'd have to follow my instincts on this one.

"Should we look for Eric?" Jeanine asked.

"No." I backed out of the driveway. "He's a man. He doesn't know where he's going."

She watched me and laughed. For the first time in a long time, I felt hopeful.

I took back roads and scanned the forest. Where could she be?

"Okay. You know your brother. Where would he keep his darkest secret?"

Jeanine gnawed on her lip. "Away from everyone else. He doesn't trust anybody."

I pulled onto the shoulder of the road. "She could be anywhere." I took another look at the map, tracing my finger along the Savannah River. "I don't know where to start."

"Well, we're going to have to start somewhere. It might as well be here."

So I turned the car off and trekked into the wilderness. For the next three hours, we looked everywhere for her. Behind every tree. Under every rock. But she wasn't there.

It was stupid of me to think finding Emily would be easy.

"It's getting dark," Jeanine gasped. "What should we do?"

"We can keep looking if you want. There are flashlights in the trunk."

"Okay," she nodded. "Yeah."

We walked back to the car only to find that it was gone.

"Umm, Addie." Jeanine rocked back on her heels. "What are we going to do?"

"I didn't park here," I said. "Everything looks different now. It's so dark."

"Now what do we do?" She crossed her arms over her chest and shivered.

"Don't freak out. We'll be fine. I know these woods."

"Then why are we lost?" She tripped over a fallen limb and screamed.

"Come on." I helped her up. "You're fine, okay? We're going to be fine."

I heard a hoot owl in the distance. Something told me to follow it. So I did.

"I have an idea." I walked into the woods and listened. When I heard the owl call to his mate, I picked up the pace. The closer I got to him, the faster my heart was beating.

When I found him at the top of a tree, the owl hooted and then took flight. I chased after him and kept my eyes on the wingspan overhead. Until I fell into the river.

"Addie!" Jeanine grabbed my arm and dragged me out. "Are you okay?"

"I'm fine." I'd had the wind knocked out of me. But as Jeanine crouched down, I spotted something over her shoulder. "Look at that."

There was an abandoned skiff hanging on the river bank. And it didn't look like anyone was coming back to claim it any time soon. While I was no thief, we were lost in the woods at night.

"Why don't you get in first?" I got up and pushed the boat into the water.

"What?" she whined. "You want me to get in that thing?"

"Don't be such a city girl. This may be our only chance to get out of here."

Jeanine peered into the river like it was a great big abyss.

"Unless you'd like to stay here all night."

It took her all of two seconds to climb into the skiff. Once she was settled, I put my back into it and pushed off the bank. Then I hopped in and grabbed a paddle.

"Get the other one." I paddled from the back end and followed the moon. It was our only source of light.

"What?" Jeanine panicked. "I don't know how to do this!"

"Well, you're just going to have to learn." I put the paddle in her hand. "It's not hard. I'll tell you everything you need to do. But you're just going to have to do it, Jeanine."

"Okay." She got a good grip on the paddle and obeyed my instructions.

We were out of sync at first, but then she got the hang of it. It was kind of a good thing we got lost, because now I could see both sides of the forest. But where was Ricky keeping her?

"Emily!" I stuck my paddle in the river to straighten the skiff out.

"Emily!" Jeanine moved to the front so our body weight would be equally distributed.

"Emily!" I looked left to right, determined to find my friend. I wasn't sure why Nicki had let Ricky's secret slip. Surely, he would kill us if he knew we were looking for Emily.

"Addie!" Jeanine shrieked and dropped her paddle. It went sinking to the bottom.

"What?" I hissed. "What is it?"

"What is that?" Her voice was shaky. "Ah!"

Jeanine saw two things. The first mesmerized her. The second terrified her.

I saw them in the same order.

There was a bright green light coming from the bottom of the river. It glowed like nothing I'd ever seen before. But I couldn't look away. It was enchanting.

"Addie!" Jeanine screamed. "Look out!"

An alligator swam in the water around us. And when he reached the light, his yellow eyes made me scream. Jeanine stood up and walked towards the back of the boat.

"No! Don't! You're gonna make us flip!"

"I'm not dying tonight!" Jeanine cried.

"Sit down and you won't!" I yelled at her like a drill sergeant. But this was life or death.

Once Jeanine took a seat, I kept still and watched the alligator out of the corner of my eye. He was circling the boat now. And the further we moved from the light, the more scared I became.

When he got too close, I hit him on the nose with the paddle—the only weapon we had. Jeanine curled into the fetal position, while I tried my best to fight him off. In the end, it wasn't good enough. The gator clamped his jaw around the paddle and chewed it to pieces.

"What do we do now?" Jeanine croaked.

The river led to a swamp where more gators awaited. I saw them in the distance and forgot how to breathe. Then I looked at the trees along the bank. And their sturdy limbs.

"Jeanine, have you ever climbed a tree before?" I asked.

Her eyes went where mine were.

"You're going to have to jump. Can you do that?"

She didn't say anything.

"Can you do that?" I yelled. "We don't have much time!"

"Yes." She was stuttering so badly she could hardly get the word out.

"Okay. On the count of three. One. Two. Three. Jump!"

I leapt out of the skiff and wrapped my limbs around a tree. But Jeanine got her foot caught in the water. I climbed down and held my arm out for her to grab.

"Take my hand!" I screamed. "Do it!"

Jeanine reached out for me and her nails dug into my skin. But I pulled her up until she got her own arms around a branch. Then we climbed to the other side and jumped down.

I ran for the hills and didn't look back. Jeanine was right behind me. And by the time we stopped for air, we must have traveled half a mile. I squatted down to catch my breath.

Jeanine ran her fingers through her hair. Sweat

was pouring down her face. We looked at each other and laughed, because it was kind of funny—how bad our luck was today.

"I thought, if I jump the gator will eat me," she said. "But if I flip the boat, Addie is going to kill me!"

We roared with laughter, no longer terrified of being eaten alive.

But then I heard a soft voice in the night.

"Addie?"

Jeanine sat up and listened.

"Addie." It was a whisper. Almost like a ghost.

I crept a few feet closer and fell to my knees.

Jeanine kept her distance, leery of coming any closer.

"What is it?" she asked.

"We found Emily."

## Chapter 19

Over two years ago. That's the last time I saw Emily alive. Now that we'd found her, I didn't know what to do.

She was cold and pale and shivering. Her hair was soaking wet. And her eyes were about as bright as a broken lamp.

"Emily." I put the back of my hand to her forehead. "Emily. Can you hear me?"

She looked up at the sky.

"Jeanine, give me your coat." I took mine off and threw it over Emily's body. "She's freezing."

Jeanine lay her coat over mine. "She looks so pale."

"Lie down beside her." I ran my hands over her arms. "She needs body heat."

"How could he do something like this?"

She was talking about her brother. That's why she couldn't say his name. She was embarrassed.

It was too much to admit out loud.

"I don't know." I lay down next to Emily and pulled her hair behind her head.

"How long do you think she's been here?" Jeanine asked.

"Days. He probably moves her so no one will know where she is."

Thunder boomed in the distance.

"Great," I said. "More rain. That's just what she needs."

"Addie," Jeanine whispered. "Shh... Someone's coming."

We lay still as I listened for footsteps. When they came, I hid Emily beneath our coats and waited. Then I closed my eyes and hoped the trees were camouflage enough.

"Addie!"

"Jeanine!"

I breathed a sigh of relief. It was only Tom. And Eric.

"Addie." Tom pulled me into his arms. "Why did you do that? It's stupid! The two of you girls in the woods by yourself?"

"I'll try to pretend that isn't sexist."

Jeanine snickered at my remark.

"You had me worried sick." Tom kissed my forehead and ran his fingers through my hair. "Don't ever do that again."

"We found her." I looked at the boys. "We found Emily."

Jeanine and I took our coats off Emily's body.

She had fallen asleep, and Eric looked like he was going to cry.

"Is she—"

"No." I checked her pulse. "She's very much alive. Just cold. Badly dehydrated. We need to take her to the hospital."

Tom tapped my shoulder so I would stop rambling. And that's when I saw tears in Eric's eyes. His lower lip was trembling as he watched over her.

"Eric, we don't have much time," I warned. "She needs help."

"Okay." He tucked a lock of hair behind Emily's ear. Then he wrapped his arm around Jeanine.

I'd never meant to be so abrupt with him. I knew how important Emily was to him. But her life was at stake. Eric would have to get over the shock later. The time to act was now.

"Where is your car?" I asked Tom.

"Just there." He pointed into the distance. "Through the trees."

"Can you carry her?" I leaned into Tom.

"I've got her." Eric picked Emily up in his arms. "Just tell me where to go."

We weaved through the thickets of the forest, unprepared for what may lie ahead. Eric lay Emily down in the back seat of his car. In all the ruckus, I'd forgotten that the boys drove separately.

"Why don't you take Jeanine and meet us there?" I told Tom. "I'm worried about Emily."

Tom looked displeased, but he accepted it. "Okay. If you'd rather ride with him."

"Could you put your jealous feelings aside for one minute?" I barked. "This is about Emily."

I turned my head when I saw something out of the corner of my eye. It was only Jeanine. She was approaching Eric's car to check on him.

In that split second, Tom grabbed my arm and pulled me behind a tree. I would have said something, but he kissed me so fast I forgot how to breathe. He cherished my lips, gifting a few kisses down my neck. As always, he left me wanting more.

"I forgot how good you were at that." I touched his cheek and smiled.

"You scared the hell out of me." There was fire in his eyes. "Don't ever do that again."

"All right," I sassed. "I heard you the first time."

He held my hand and walked me to Eric's car. I got in the back seat and cradled Emily's head in my lap. Even now, she was still shivering.

It was summer in Savannah.

So why was she so cold?

We drove to the hospital, and Emily was admitted immediately. On the ride over, she went into anaphylactic shock. It was a good thing I was in the back seat with her. Eric nearly crashed the car.

After a few hours, a doctor came to see us. He knew Eleanor and Eric's parents. Finally, my adoptive mother's time-sucking occupation proved useful.

"She's malnourished and severely dehydrated," the doctor said. "Some hypothermia."

"She's been missing," Eric reminded him.

"I know." The doctor looked at us funny. "Where did you find her?"

"In the woods," I said.

He clenched his jaw. "Any idea who put her there?"

We didn't say anything. Jeanine and Tom were across the room. They were close enough to hear, but they kept their mouths shut. Quite frankly, we didn't know what to say.

"I don't know," Eric muttered. "When can she go home?"

"Son, I know what you've been through. But you've got to give her time to rest."

"Well, I'm checking her out. Tonight. My parents don't need to see this."

I didn't think it was wise. But there was no fighting Eric. So she left with us that night.

Eric's family may have bought a house in Savannah. But it wasn't furnished yet. There was no food or a fridge. So we all drove out to my house instead.

First of all, there was plenty of room—*and* food. And Eleanor was a doctor. So if anything happened, Emily would have medical care of some kind. That is, if Eleanor ever took time off from her Medical Conventions World Tour.

Eric put Emily in the guest room upstairs where she could rest. Tom went into the kitchen to reheat dinner for everyone. And Jeanine walked the halls biting her nails off to the quick.

When Eric came downstairs, we ate in silence. No one wanted to wake Emily. And Eric rushed back to her side before he was done.

At the hospital, he'd called Mr. and Mrs. Kent. I couldn't imagine what they must be going through. They were driving overnight from Atlanta. But I knew they wanted to be here sooner.

Around two a.m. everyone decided it was time to go to bed. Eric stayed in Emily's room, while Tom headed upstairs with me. Jeanine had already volunteered to stay on the couch downstairs. She said after a day like this, she needed the TV on to sleep.

Tom locked the door and then took off his shirt. As he stalked towards me, I snuggled beneath the covers. He joined me and touched my face.

"I'm gonna marry you one day."

"Tom." I went to slap his arm, but he grabbed my hand.

"No, I mean it." He rearranged a lock of hair until it framed my face. "I can't believe Ricky is alive."

I raised my brow.

"You thought I forgot about that?"

"No." I put my hand on his chest. "I don't

know how or why. But he *is* alive."

"What he did to you." He tightened his arms around me. "Do you think he did that to her, too?"

I nodded.

And then I cried. Long sobs—the gut wrenching kind. All this time, we'd thought Emily was dead. In the past two years, there were probably times she'd wished she had been.

That's how I fell asleep that night—crying in Tom's arms. He was good at soothing me. Rubbing my back and shoulders, whispering into my neck.

When I dozed off, his arms were wrapped around me tight. I felt safe and warm. Until I had one of those damn nightmares again. Would they ever go away?

I think it was around four a.m. when I knew something was wrong. Tom was sound asleep beside me. But I could feel it in the air.

So I slipped out of bed to use the bathroom. Despite my exhaustion, I was on edge. My heart wouldn't stop racing.

I washed my hands in the sink and looked at my reflection. I saw Ricky in the mirror and gasped. But when I turned around, he was gone.

"You're fine," I whispered. "Breathe. It's all in your head."

I thought about getting back in bed with Tom. But I was so riled up now, that it defeated the purpose. So I tiptoed out of my bedroom to check on everyone.

Leaning into the banister, I watched Jeanine sleeping on the couch downstairs. The TV was still on, but the volume was too low for anyone to hear. So I marked her as *safe* in my mind and went on to the next house guest.

Eric was snoring in a chair, but it brought a smile to my face. Even though these were loud grizzly bear snores I was hearing. They had yet to disturb Emily and that was all that mattered.

Seeing her alive gave me so much happiness. My best friend was back from the dead. And I was dying to tell her everything she'd missed while she was gone.

Especially about Tom. While Jeanine was my friend, it wasn't the same as spilling my guts to Emily. Jeanine and Tom were related. Sometimes, that complicated things.

As I reminisced over our time together, something felt weird. I reached Emily to get an up close look. And that's when reality struck me right in the face.

Like Mike Tyson in a boxing match.

Emily was dead.

# Chapter 20

S tone cold. That's how her skin felt. Like a block of ice.

But she couldn't be dead. She just couldn't be. Something was wrong.

I opened her eyelids, checked her pulse. She wasn't breathing. Her chest was still.

Nothing made sense. We had just taken her to the hospital. Wouldn't the doctor have said something? Made her stay overnight?

And then I saw it. Like a dagger in my heart.

There was a drop of blood on her pillow. I looked closer and closer, zooming my eyes in like a microscope. More blood. A gash on the back of her head. One that hadn't been there before.

Cold air blew into the room, and a chill crawled up my spine. Before bed, Tom had said something about setting the thermostat. But my air conditioning wasn't known for emitting gusts of wind in the middle of the night.

I turned around and gulped. The window was open. The same one I'd just walked by. Two minutes ago, it was closed. And that could only mean one thing.

A cold hand clamped over my mouth. "Don't make a sound."

His arm tightened around my waist. I felt him behind me, breathing down my neck.

"You lied to me, Addie." His fingertips sank into my skin. "You gave me the wrong necklace."

When I whimpered, he squeezed so tight I couldn't breathe. I looked at Emily in the bed. He pressed his head against mine, seamlessly reading my mind.

"I didn't have a choice," he said. "You took her to the hospital. And I couldn't let her regain consciousness. She could identify me. We couldn't let that happen."

He walked me to the end of the bed, where Eric was sound asleep. I shut my eyes and let the tears pour out of me. If only he'd been a light sleeper. Eric could take Ricky down in a minute. I was sure of it. But none of that mattered now.

"You're coming with me. Quietly. Or I'll just have to kill them, too."

I nodded against his chest, agreeing to whatever I had to. As he took me out of the bedroom, I looked back at Eric. Then we moved down the hall, and he stalled in front of the door to my bedroom. I kept still, praying that he wouldn't peek inside.

But Ricky steered me in that direction. "Is your precious boyfriend in there?" He slid his hand under my shirt. "Sleeping in your bed tonight?"

I pushed his hand away and he pinned my arms to my chest. Then he crept towards the door I'd left cracked. When he pressed his palm to the wood, it squeaked open.

Tom was on his side, facing the window. His arm hung over my side of the bed. The warm spot I had just left. Now, I was wishing I had woken him up with me.

There was a noise down below. Ricky looked back and then held me against the banister. It was my only saving grace—Jeanine talking in her sleep.

The TV was still on, but she was lost in a dream. Ricky eased me down the staircase, while I watched *Titanic* on the screen. Leo was freezing in the water. So blue he was white.

Somehow, I thought Ricky seeing his sister might change his mind. If Jeanine couldn't shift his focal point, then nothing could. And that's when I realized there was no going back.

He took me out the back door and threw me on the ground. My cheek hit the dirt as he tied my hands behind my back. Out of the corner of my eye, I saw Tom in the window.

Then Ricky hit me in the head. And everything went black.

\* \* \*

When I woke up, it wasn't like last time. I was woozier. And for a second, I forgot who I was. Everything sounded like music in my ears. Vibrations instead of voices.

I was on a slab of concrete with my back to the wall. I was tired. I was cold.

Ricky jerked me up and hauled me across the room. The place looked like an old basement. The lights were dim. And there was a leak in the ceiling.

But that wasn't the strangest thing about my prison. There was a projector set up in the back of the room. Like the kind my teachers used in middle school.

While Ricky was tying me to a chair, DeMilo walked into the room. Hugh was next. He took a seat and rolled a cigarette. Then he struck a match and looked into my eyes.

I remembered the night he tied me to a tree. The night he blew smoke in my mouth. The night he kissed me. I also remembered him telling DeMilo he was married once.

Poor wife.

"What are you doing?" I looked up at Ricky. But I was too groggy to be afraid.

He cracked a smile, crossing his arms over his chest. "You lied to me."

"No." I shook my head slowly. "This is over. I gave you the necklace."

DeMilo approached me and pulled the

necklace out of his pocket.

"Yeah, that's it. What do you want now? I found the necklace. I gave you what you wanted."

"This necklace is a fake," DeMilo said. Then he tossed it in my lap.

"How do you know that?" I asked. "Jimmy gave it to me."

DeMilo grinned. "Well, aren't we quick to throw our father under the bus?"

"He's not my father!" I hung my head. For some reason, I felt ashamed.

"Is that what he told you?" DeMilo walked to the wall and looked at Ricky.

"Yeah," I admitted. "I really wanted him to be. I wanted to believe you."

Ricky put a photograph on the projector. Ripped out of a history book.

"Are you familiar with Marie Antoinette?" DeMilo asked.

"What?" I looked between him and Ricky. Then I watched Hugh.

"Marie Antoinette. Do you know who she is?"

"Umm. Yeah," I swallowed. "But what does that have to do with—"

"Why don't you shut your mouth for a change and listen?" DeMilo said.

I sank into my chair, feeling bruised by his scolding. Then again, some of the bruises were probably real.

"Antoinette was only fifteen when she married Louis XVI."

"Yes," I interrupted. "The same age as your granddaughter, Jeanine."

I thought that would faze him. And while he stopped for a second, the mention of her name hadn't produced the desired effect. Maybe he didn't care about her. Or Tom.

"She was the queen of France." DeMilo pointed at the portrait. "Before the French Revolution, there was an incident in 1785—The Affair of the Diamond Necklace."

I pulled at the rope around my wrists and saw Hugh smoking in the corner.

"Have you ever heard of it?" DeMilo stood in front of the projector until he had my full attention.

"No." I shook my head. "I don't know what it is."

DeMilo gestured to Ricky, who put another photo on the projector.

"It was a diamond necklace commissioned for Madame du Barry. She was a favorite mistress of King Louis XV. But he died in 1774 before the necklace was complete."

I shifted in my seat and swallowed. There was a metallic taste in my mouth, and I was starting to sweat. A fan would have been nice at a time like this. But I didn't see one.

"A few years later, the jewelers who made the necklace hoped Marie Antoinette would buy it. But when she refused, several other players stepped into the picture."

Ricky dropped a book on the projector. He flipped from page to page. All the faces blurred together so fast, I couldn't make any of them out.

"Essentially, the necklace created a scandal. Morale was weak. And the people could see it. Some say, it led to the French Revolution. You know what they did to the Queen?"

DeMilo could be so smug. Then again, he was always smug. I didn't see the need for the history lesson, but it was smarter to play along. So I did.

"They cut off her head." I fluttered my lashes. "Or do you prefer the term decapitation?"

DeMilo snickered. "You're a clever girl. That's why I've always found you so useful."

I stared at the ground and remembered seeing Tom in the window. He must have woken up, which meant he knew Ricky had taken me. And he was on his way here right now. Only, where was *here*? How would Tom be able to find me?

"But what history won't tell you is that Marie Antoinette found a way to survive." DeMilo walked over to the projector and closed the history book. "The Parisian jewelers felt responsible for her appointment with the guillotine. So they hired an alchemist to fashion her a new necklace. An emerald necklace."

Ricky put a picture of Marie Antoinette on the projector. She was wearing the necklace.

"One that would protect her from evil, harm, even death. A talisman."

"Well, it must not be very good. I mean, they

executed her anyway."

"Two weeks before her trial, someone stole the necklace," DeMilo said. "That's why she died. It had nothing to do with the guillotine."

I eyed DeMilo and then looked at the men in the room. Were they really buying this?

"So you're telling me the necklace would have saved her?" I asked. "That—if she'd been wearing it—they wouldn't have been able to execute her? That the guillotine—"

"It's not magic, you know." DeMilo coughed. "It would have saved her."

My head was spinning. I was thirsty and confused. Not to mention, uncomfortable.

Days ago, I truly believed it was over. DeMilo had what he wanted. There was no reason to ever bother me again. Tonight felt like one big misunderstanding.

"Okay. So you're saying my grandmother's necklace is like Marie Antoinette's?"

"No." DeMilo pulled up a chair and sat down. "It *is* Marie Antoinette's."

You could hear a pin drop in that dark, dank room. I couldn't wrap my head around what was happening. Was I in the Twilight Zone or something?

"It's the same one," DeMilo said. "And I need it."

"But you said I gave you a fake?" I narrowed my eyes.

"You did. And now I need you to give me the

real one."

"I did give you the real one. That's the only one I have!"

"No." He shook his head. "You gave me a fake. It doesn't work."

"I don't know where it is, Tony." I stared at him. "I don't have it."

Ricky slapped me, and I felt my jaw pop. I was seeing stars by the time I saw DeMilo walking away. His history lesson kept running through my head. There was a piece missing.

"If that necklace really did belong to Marie Antoinette, then how did my grandmother get it?" That stopped DeMilo in his tracks. "Just because her name was Antoinette, too?"

"Your grandmother was a descendant of French aristocracy. And so are you."

I pinched my eyebrows together. Why couldn't he just spell it out for me? I was tired of trying to put the puzzle pieces together. He needed to stop tiptoeing around the truth.

But the silence made me think. And suddenly everything was clear to me.

"Am I...?" I looked at the projector screen. "Was she...?"

"Yes, you're related to Marie Antoinette and King Louis. You're French Royalty, really. But I'd only consider them distant relatives. Since it's been over two hundred years."

My jaw dropped, and there was a deadly smile on his face. I couldn't breathe.

"No." I refused it. "I couldn't be—I'm not related to a queen!"

"I'm tired of playing games with you, child." DeMilo put his jacket on. "We'll all go into the woods tonight. You have until sunrise to show me where the necklace is."

"I don't have it!" I cried.

"Okay then. Wherever you've hidden it."

Tears ran down my face. He wouldn't believe me. But I was telling the truth.

"You have twelve hours." He set a timer. "And then the hunt begins."

When he left, Ricky untied me. Then he threw the ropes on the ground and took a seat. After everything he'd done, I wasn't even scared of him. I was more afraid of the hunt. Whatever that entailed.

"Don't worry about it too much," Ricky said. "He's just afraid of dying."

"What?" I hardly registered the words.

"He has syphilis." Ricky kept his eyes on me. "Didn't you know?"

I shook my head.

"Well, that's why. He's not normally like this. He's actually a pretty cool guy."

"How long have you known that he was your grandfather?" I asked.

Ricky averted his eyes, like he couldn't look at me. "The dance."

I furrowed my brow. That didn't sound right. "Prom?"

"No." He shook his head. "The one before that. When you wore that white dress."

I thought about that night. It was the first time I met Tom. At the time, I'd thought it was all a dream. Because Ricky had attempted to abduct me that night. Or so Tom said.

I was sure the memory was up there, but it never came back to me. For the first time, I wondered if Ricky was as bad as I'd remembered. Or had it always been about DeMilo?

Was it all for his grandfather? An attempt to save his life?

"I thought syphilis was treatable. My mom is a doctor, you know."

"I know you're not stupid," Ricky said. "You're one of the smartest girls I know."

Something inside me fluttered from the compliment. Maybe it was because he was finally acting the way I'd always wanted him to. Like a gentleman. Like Tom.

He stood up. "He's got a different kind. It's rare. Some other strand." On his feet, he tugged at his belt and looked down at me. "Anyway, it's fatal. No doctor can save him."

"But—"

"Trust me, he's been to all of them. And they don't know what it is. They say they can't do anything for him. He's known for a while now."

"How long?" I wasn't asking how long he'd known. I was asking how long he had left.

Ricky smoldered. "Three weeks."

For a moment, I almost felt sorry for Ricky. I wanted to reach out and touch him. But then I realized what kind of dream I was having. One that was very real.

"Why did you do it?" Rage ignited within me. Everything was coming back.

"What?"

"Emily," I moaned. "You had no reason to take her. Why did you do it?"

He towered over me. His eyes looked like whiskey. He stared at my mouth.

"You're sure you want to know?" He lowered himself to my level.

I nodded.

"I thought she was you."

He walked away taking every last ounce of hope with him.

And then I remembered what I hadn't had enough time to forget.

Emily was dead.

## Chapter 21

They kept me inside all day. I wasn't allowed to eat or drink. Bathroom breaks were infrequent but not strictly prohibited. And for that I was grateful.

Tom had yet to break down the door and rescue me. But this wasn't a fairy tale. Tom may have been a good boyfriend. But he wasn't Prince Charming. No one was going to help me. If I wanted rescuing, I was going to have to save myself.

There was a small window in the basement. It was frosted glass, so I couldn't see outside. But it let in enough light for me to tell when the sun was setting.

Hugh must have gone through two packs of cigarettes by now. The men played cards and drank booze. While I was confined to the chair. Since his history lecture, DeMilo had yet to make an appearance. Maybe he was resting in the back. Preparing for tonight.

As the clock ticked, I came up with a plan. Surely, I knew the woods better than them. DeMilo was a city boy from New York. And Ricky had spent more time on the football field than the outskirts of town. Then again, he'd learned his way around the wilderness enough to keep Emily hidden for two years.

In reality, I had no idea what I was up against. They always threatened to kill me. It was a constant staple hanging over my head. But if there was no necklace, would they?

If DeMilo really believed I could find it, then why would he get rid of me? Maybe the best course of action was to show them nothing. If DeMilo chose to eliminate me, he would be killing any chance of recovery.

It would be the closest thing to penning his own suicide note.

Kill me, and DeMilo was as good as dead.

When it was time to leave, they put a bag over my head. I should have expected treatment like this, but I was in such a daze. Maybe it was the head injury I had sustained.

They stuffed me in the back seat of a car. I was just happy it wasn't a trunk.

As I heard tires rolling over gravel, I thought about my first time. When DeMilo confined me to a cave and Hugh practiced Chinese water torture on me in the river. The memory sent a shiver down my spine. My experiences with these men were like armor.

They had prepared me for tonight.

When the car stopped, my throat went dry. Despite my bravery, I certainly wasn't comfortable with the situation. But like always, I didn't see where I had much of a choice.

Ricky took the bag off my head. "Stay with me." He rubbed my wrists once he removed the ropes. And I couldn't react to his tenderness with anything other than bewilderment.

"Why?" I whispered so DeMilo wouldn't hear.

"Because I have a plan to get us both out of here. Alive."

There was a full moon hanging in the sky. One night. That was all I had to find the necklace and send DeMilo on his way. Hopefully, he would be out of my life forever.

"Why should I trust you?" I looked up at him. "You're a murderer and a rapist."

Ricky looked over his shoulder and tugged at my arm. Since Hugh and DeMilo were nearby, I followed him behind a tree where we could talk privately.

"Run away with me," he said.

"What?" My head snapped back. "You must be joking."

"No." He touched my face. "I'm serious."

"I'm just trying to stay alive, okay? I'm not going anywhere with you."

"I'll make sure he lets you live." He pointed at

DeMilo.

"Oh, so you can kill me yourself?" I huffed.

He squeezed my hands. "Run away with me. I promise you'll like it."

"*Why* would I run away with you?" I pushed him back. "Have you forgotten all the times you attacked me? Nearly raped me? The only reason I'm standing here talking to you right now is because I guess I'm more afraid of your grandfather than you."

"I was drunk—anytime I've ever tried to hurt you."

I slapped him and took a little pleasure in it. "Like when you did that?"

He laughed, rubbing his cheek. "Yeah, I guess so. I never meant to—"

"What about Tom?" I narrowed my eyes. "I don't want to leave him."

"Well." Ricky tilted his head. "He can learn to live without you."

I balled my hand into a fist and clenched my jaw. If he thought I was never going to see Tom again, that I was going to run away with him instead, he was insane.

"What if I don't want to live without him?" I asked.

He backed me up against a tree. "You'll learn to like it."

I heard something and turned my head. But Ricky dove at the opportunity to kiss me. His fingers were in my hair, unwelcome and unwanted.

He was a rough, sloppy kisser.

"Get off me!" I pushed him away and Hugh approached.

"What are you doing?" Hugh looked between us.

"Nothing." Ricky kept his eyes on me.

I shook it off and tried to forget the kiss. My hands were balled into fists. But I pushed my anger aside. If I was going to survive the night, I needed endurance on my side.

Once we entered the wilderness, I paid attention to the trees. Ricky volunteered to guard me at the back of the group, while everyone else went on ahead. I wanted to complain, but who was going to listen? It wasn't like they had an HR Department.

"Run away with me," he pushed.

I kept walking and gave him the silent treatment. So this was how the next few hours were going to be. DeMilo was ready to murder me. And Ricky was prepared to save me.

"Come on, Addie." Ricky wrapped his arm around me. "You wouldn't have to worry about school, work or money ever again. You can forget the life you have here."

"I like my life, Ricky." I eased out of his hold. "I don't want to forget it."

He stood still and let me go on without him. But it was too good to be true.

"If Tom really loves you, he would care more about you being alive."

I rolled my eyes and watched an owl fly overhead. "You're not making any sense."

"Don't you think he'd rather you be alive than dead?" he asked.

"Yes."

"If you run away with me, you'll be alive. You'll be safe."

"But would he know that?" I couldn't believe I was even considering it.

"It would probably be better if he didn't."

"Why?" I got in his face. "So you can have a new captive?"

"I didn't *want* to kill Emily," he said. "I had to. She could have identified me."

"You already told me that." I tripped and he caught me. But I was repulsed.

"Why do you hate me so much?"

I stopped in my tracks. "The fact that you even have to ask me that says a lot."

"So I'm a sadist and a sociopath. So what? That doesn't mean we can't be happy."

"When are you going to get it through your thick skull?" I gritted my teeth, but kept my voice down. I didn't want the others to hear. "I'm never going to *love* you. I'm never going to *be* with you. I'm never going to *want* you. Tom is it for me. My first and last."

"That's pretty close-minded. I mean, you're only seventeen. You don't even know what else is out there." He walked backwards beside me. "You haven't even tried it."

"Maybe I don't want to try it!"

"I do love you, Addie." He touched my arm. "I just wish you would let me."

"I'm not sure I like your idea of love," I scowled. "And I sure don't want it."

He shoved his hands in his pockets and stayed quiet for a few minutes. But his presence was like a stitch in my side. He was pulling at the thread, digging deeper.

"What's so great about him?" he asked.

I took a deep breath through my nose. How far were we going to walk? Hadn't DeMilo figured out by now that I didn't have a clue where the necklace was? I didn't want to know.

"Why do you like him?" Ricky pressed. "Why do you like Tom?"

"Because he's a good guy. And I find that very attractive."

"Really?" He looked taken aback.

"Sorry to disappoint you, but I don't like bad boys."

He curled his lip at me. "But it feels so good to be bad."

"Well, you would know."

"Are you sleeping with him?" He moved closer.

I looked at him and glared. "That's none of your business!"

"Then I guess that's a no."

"My sex life is *none* of your business," I reinforced.

"I love you. And you're going to be mine. So yes, it is my business."

"Stop saying you love me! You don't know what love is."

"Oh, and you do. You and your Tom, who is *such* a gentleman."

"Yes," I growled. "He is. What's wrong with that?"

"Nothing. That's just not how I do business."

Business. How romantic. Who talks like that about love and sex?

"If you're so in love with me, what about Nicki?" I asked.

"Nicki?"

"Yeah. You never stopped to think about her? Nicki *loves* you."

"Yeah, well that's her problem."

"Do you even hear yourself? You're the reason she's such a mess and semi-suicidal! How many times have you gotten her pregnant?"

He stopped and grabbed my arm. I was being stupid—engaging in a comfortable conversation with him. Thinking he was normal enough to be laid back. And not try to hurt me.

"How do you know about that?" he rasped.

"Let go of my arm." He was squeezing so tightly, my skin was starting to sting.

"Who told you about that? No one is supposed to know about that!"

"Let go of my arm!" I cried and fell on the ground when he released me.

The ruckus caused a stir in the group. Just enough to make DeMilo turn around. "What's going on?" he asked. "And where the hell are we going?"

"Just keep walking," Ricky said. "We need to get deeper in the forest."

I looked up at them from the flat of my back. They towered over me.

"It's buried back there." Ricky helped me up. "That's what she said."

I had no idea where he was going with this. But I kept up pretenses.

"Addie, is that right?" DeMilo asked.

Ricky dug his nails into my arm.

"Yes," I winced. "Yeah, that's right."

"How much farther?" DeMilo eyed me curiously. Like a snake.

"Not too far," Ricky answered for me.

I nodded, but I had no idea why I was trusting him.

When the men walked off, Ricky waited a beat and then dragged me through the trees. Before I could scream, he had me pinned to the ground beneath him. He put his hand over my mouth. And then he looked over his shoulder until the group was gone.

"I'm going to let you go, but you have to be quiet," he said.

I didn't say a word. I wanted him to fulfill his end of the bargain. When he did, I almost died of shock. But Ricky helped me to my feet and took my hand.

"I can get you out of here." He kissed me. "I promise I'll keep you safe."

"Ricky, wait." I pulled back against him. "What are you talking about?"

"We can leave. Tonight." He lifted my chin. "Before they know we're gone."

I shook my head. "How?"

"I know where the necklace is."

## Chapter 22

**H**ow do you know where the necklace is?" I let go of his hand.

"I can't tell you." He touched my back. "You're just going to have to trust me."

Trust my enemy? Why did that seem to be a reoccurring theme lately?

"Okay." I agreed to it blindly. "Fine."

He kissed me on the cheek. He looked genuinely happy. I was just playing along.

I didn't want his hands all over me. But I might have to tolerate it for a night. If that was the only way to see Tom again—to make it out of here alive—then it was a misfortune I was willing to endure.

"Come on." Ricky dragged me behind him. "We have to hurry."

I felt dizzy as we ran through the trees. I heard the hoot owl again. It made me sick.

All I really wanted was to go home. I wanted to crawl into bed with Tom and never wake up. I wanted him to hold me close and tell me that everything was going to be all right. But Tom wasn't here right now.

Tonight wasn't about getting what I wanted. To save myself, I would have to let Ricky get what *he* wanted. I could pretend it was Tom. As long as I survived until morning.

When we reached the river, déjà vu washed over me. Hadn't I just been here?

"Dammit!" Ricky searched the bank. "Where's the boat?"

"What boat?" I played dumb. Stupid and blonde were my new allies.

"My boat!" Ricky motioned at the empty ground. "I had a boat here!"

"What happened to it?" I asked.

"I don't know!"

Ricky could be really scary when he wanted to. I shivered and closed my eyes.

I knew where we were. And I knew where the boat was. But he didn't.

"Why do we need a boat anyway?" I rubbed his shoulder. "Can't we just get on the road? We should take the car and leave. You know how to hotwire a car, right?"

"Yes, I know how to hotwire a car!" He withdrew from me. "That's not the point."

"Then what is the point, Ricky? You were the one who wanted to run away together."

He lifted his head. "I thought you didn't."

"Well, maybe I've changed my mind." I put my hand on his chest and smiled.

"Oh, Addie." He cradled my face in his hands. Then he leaned in and put his mouth on mine. I didn't like it. If I'm being perfectly honest, I hated it. But I pretended to love it.

"As long as Tom is safe." I touched his face. "And he knows I'm alive."

"Okay." He looped his arms around my waist. "But he can't know where you are."

I accepted his conditions. And he kissed me again.

"There's something else." Ricky put his hand on my shoulder. A little too much like a predator, if you ask me. "If we do this, you can never leave. You must always stay with me."

"What?"

"If you run—if you try to leave me." He put his hand around my throat. "I'll kill you myself."

I gulped and took a breath, falling to the ground when he released me. I didn't know what I was getting into. I wasn't prepared for this. Where was Tom?

"You." I heard a shaky voice from behind. "How could you?"

Nicki came out from the shadows. There were tears running down her face.

"You lied to me!" I thought she was talking to Ricky. But she was staring at me.

"Nicki, I—"

"You said you loved Tom. You said—"

"Addie and I are running away together," Ricky interrupted. "You can't come along."

She took a step back and lost her breath. Then she crumpled to the ground.

I wanted to reach out and help her. But Ricky held me back.

"Get out of here, Nicki!" Ricky pointed into the distance. "Leave us alone."

She was on her knees. "Please Ricky. Take me with you."

"No. I don't want to take you with me. I want Addie."

Watching him say those things to her was torture. Despite my history with Nicki, I knew she loved him. It was so cruel for him to treat her like a dog on the street.

"I can't survive without you," she cried. "I won't be able to."

"I don't care!" Ricky spit on the ground. "I don't want you anymore."

"No," she moaned. "Not again."

"Addie is the girl I love." He squeezed my waist. "She always has been."

When Nicki heard that, it was like he cut her in two. She hung her head and wept, crying and sobbing over a life she would never have. Personally, I thought Nicki was too good for him. Her best shot at a good life was with someone else.

Why couldn't she see that?

"Where will you go? What will you do?" Her

teeth were chattering.

"I don't know." Ricky held me close. "We'll think of something."

I wanted to squirm and shove him off me. But that would wipe away the façade I'd been working so hard to construct. If Ricky believed me, then I could count on the possibility of escape. Moments would arise. Opportunities would present themselves.

And I would take them.

"I won't let you go!" Nicki crawled to his feet. "I can't!"

"Nicki, you need to go home," he said. "Forget about me."

"Did you ever love me?" She looked up at him. "At all."

"In a way, I guess. But never like this. Never like it is with Addie."

I averted my eyes. She must have hated me. But what could I do?

She wanted to be in his arms as badly as I wanted to leave them. But I couldn't crack the façade, the clever exterior I'd built up. Ricky needed to believe I would go with him willingly. It was the only way to gain his trust. So I could finally break free.

"What's so special about her?" Nicki asked. "Why do you like her so much?"

"I don't know." Ricky was getting frustrated. "I just do."

"Then why didn't you tell me? I would have

done whatever you wanted, been whoever you wanted, said whatever you wanted me to say. Ricky, I just—"

"I don't want a Barbie doll, Nicki. You of all people should know that by now."

Something about those last words really rubbed her the wrong way. Nicki rose from the ground with mud on her face and hands. She looked at me, and I saw her eye twitch.

In the span of a minute, she snapped. And I— the sacrificial lamb—paid the price.

"You don't love me anymore?" she asked Ricky.

He sighed. "I don't think I've ever loved you."

In one swift move, Nicki lunged for me and clawed my cheek with her nails. I cried out and touched my cheek. There were scratches on my face. There was blood.

Ricky stepped between us and shoved her off me. While I was thankful for his protection, Ricky was the root of the problem. He shouldn't have said those things to her. Now Nicki would hate me forever. That is, if she didn't kill me first.

"You said you would always love me!" she screamed. "You lied!"

Nicki pounced on him as I staggered back. My butt hit the ground, while the rest of reality gave way. I looked on in horror as she climbed on top of Ricky and hit him.

They rolled on the ground, and I wondered if it was a good opportunity to run. But then Ricky got the upper hand, sliding her body beneath his. When she fought against him, Ricky dragged her body over the bank and dunked her head in the river.

"Ricky! No!" I climbed on his back as he tried to drown her.

When I kicked him in the kidney, Ricky fell to his side. He released his death grip on Nicki, and I breathed a sigh of relief. Until she grabbed my hair and pulled me underwater.

I flailed around in the murky river, grabbing at the rocks. But Nicki came after me in a jealous rage. Just when I held my head above water, she pulled me back under again.

I was sucking water down like a vacuum cleaner. And there seemed to be no way to stop it. When I coughed, my lungs burned with discomfort. It was unbearable.

Ricky grabbed my hand and pulled me above the surface. As I hung on for dear life, Nicki came up behind me. I saw a knife in her hand and elbowed her in the head.

But it was a harsh blow. Her eyes rolled back into her head. And she sank to the bottom.

Terror flashed in Ricky's eyes, and he dove in the water after her. I dragged myself onto the bank and lay down. Now would have been the perfect time to flee—with both of them underwater. But my lungs were just so tired. I could hardly breathe.

When Ricky emerged, he put her body on the ground and checked her pulse. Then he administered CPR. Pumping her chest. Breathing into her mouth. Pumping again.

He was cursing and crying. If I'd known he really cared about her, I would have manipulated him into running away with her instead. But Ricky was the one who kept driving home the point—that I was the one he wanted.

But was I? Really?

Ricky leaned back on the bank. He was out of breath.

"She's dead."

I looked at her corpse. Cold. White. Her eyes were still open. So Ricky shut them and kissed her for the last time. Then he scooped up her body and placed her in the river.

My mouth hung open in shock as she floated downstream. It was the image of a fallen angel. I didn't know what to do or say. We'd had our disagreements in the past. But I didn't hate Nicki. And I certainly hadn't wished for her death.

"You killed her," Ricky said.

"What?" I leaned my head back in fear of him.

"You killed her," he repeated. "You killed her. You killed her. You killed her."

"No, I didn't. She was trying to drown me."

"I did love her." He got down on his knees. "What have you done?"

"I didn't do anything." I stood up and took a few steps back.

"Now she's gone." He gazed downstream, but she wasn't there.

"I didn't kill Nicki," I said. "You were the one with your hands around her throat."

"You killed her." He pushed me back in the river. "How could you?"

I tried to swim away, but he grabbed my hair. Then he pushed down on my shoulders until my head was under the water. I held on to his arms, clawing at his shirt—anything to pull myself up. But Ricky was never one for showing mercy.

Especially if you were someone who needed it.

"Ricky!" I choked on water. "Ricky! Stop!"

But he kept dunking my head in the water. And when he wrapped his hands around my throat, I knew I was a goner. My whole body was shaking, and my chest was on fire.

A flash of light went over my eyes like an electric shock. It was white hot.

I felt the world caving in on me as the life left my hands. Ricky was bringing me to heel, sucking every last breath out of me. And when the last was gone, it felt like I was floating.

When I sprang awake, water was climbing up my throat. I leaned over the edge of the bank and coughed it up. Even though my throat was already bruised and sore.

"Breathe," he said. "Breathe, baby. Breathe."

I opened my eyes, and Tom was there. He ran his fingers through my hair, leaving kisses on my forehead. I fell into his arms and cried, holding on especially tight.

"Don't let go," I whimpered. "*Please.* Don't let

go."

He cradled my body against him. "I'll never let go."

"What happened to Ricky?" I squeezed Tom in my arms.

"He's unconscious." But as we looked around, he was nowhere to be found.

"Tom." Ricky was gone. And that scared me.

I felt a shadow looming and screamed when Ricky swung a metal bat over my head. Tom shielded my body and then dragged me away. But Ricky was coming closer, striking the ground in front of me with the bat every time he missed my face.

All of a sudden, Eric came out of the woods and tackled Ricky to the ground. When I screamed, Tom picked me up in his arms and set me down in front of the trees. He was headed over there, so I grabbed his leg and pulled him back to me.

"No!" I cried. "Don't go!"

Tom crouched down and held me in his arms, while we watched Eric beat Ricky to a pulp. There was blood everywhere. And when it was clear that Ricky wouldn't be able to stand, Eric got up and grabbed the bat. He held it over his head and I closed my eyes.

"No!" Jeanine appeared from the forest. "Eric, don't!"

"He killed my sister," Eric said.

Jeanine looked between the two of them and

sobbed. "But he's my brother."

When Eric raised the bat, I burrowed a hole in Tom's chest. He covered my eyes.

"NOOOOOOOO!!!!!!!!!!!!!!!"

It happened so fast. There was a loud crack. And then Jeanine screamed in agony.

Tom held me in his lap as I wrapped my arms around him. I was shaking.

Eric dropped the bat and rinsed the blood off his hands in the river. Then he crouched down to comfort Jeanine. But she was rocking back and forth.

"Get away from me!" She shoved his shoulder. "Don't touch me. Don't *touch* me!"

Eric stood up and looked at us. Then he hung his head and walked away.

"He had to do it," Tom whispered so only I could hear. "He had to."

Jeanine crawled to the river's edge and put her hand in the water. Then she lay down on the bank and stared at the sky. I was worried about her. Was she going into shock?

"You're so cold." Tom rubbed his hands over my back. "I don't want you to be cold."

"I want to go home." I nuzzled his neck. "Take me home."

"I can't do that," he said.

Confused, I leaned back in his lap. "Why not?"

He cradled my face in his hands and smiled. Then he put his forehead to mine. It was a whisper against my lips. But I heard him loud and clear.

"I found the necklace."

## Chapter 23

I looked at him like he'd just spoken in French. Why had I been hearing that a lot lately? Every one kept claiming they had found the necklace. I wished it didn't exist.

"Maybe we should just get out of here." I glanced at Ricky's body on the ground. "Leave."

"No." Tom cupped my cheek in his hand. "I want it to be over with them. Finished."

I nodded and turned back. Jeanine crawled on her hands and knees to get to Ricky. He was flat on his back, and there was a pool of blood on the ground beneath his head. Despite the past few months, I had a pretty good feeling that this time, he was really dead.

"Jeanine." I saw the pain in her eyes. "Come on. We have to go."

"No," she wept. "I don't want to leave him."

"You'll see him again." Tom knelt down to

close Ricky's eyes. "I promise."

I grabbed her shoulders. "We have to give DeMilo the necklace and get out of here. So we can finally be done with this." I lifted her chin. "And you can go back to a normal life."

"Normal?" Her lower lip trembled. "How can you ever think my life will be normal after this?" She gazed at her brother's face and stroked his cheek tenderly.

On her behalf, there was genuine love there. No matter how evil he was, Jeanine didn't want him to die. I guess what all the old folks say is true. *Blood is thicker than water.*

When we convinced Jeanine to move, Tom led us down the river bank. She kept looking back to make sure Ricky's body was still there. And I promised her that we would return to see that he had a proper burial. My loyalty was with Emily. But this was for Jeanine.

Tom came to an abrupt stop and I slammed into his back. He stuck his arm out to shield us with his body. And then he told us to move away from the bank.

That was when I saw it again—the bright green light. It radiated from the bottom of the river. Just like it had when Jeanine and I were in the boat. But then I remembered what else we had seen, too. Alligators. And from the looks of it, they had multiplied.

"Umm. Tom." I tugged his shirtsleeve. "I don't think we should be here."

"There he is!" Jimmy emerged from the woods with DeMilo. "He knows where it is."

Hugh walked out next, a lit cigarette in hand. I leaned into Tom, feeling protective over the man I loved. Blood pounded through me at the betrayal. I couldn't believe it.

"Jimmy?" I looked him up and down. "What are you doing here?"

"You didn't really think I was your father, did you?" He came up to me. "What did I tell you? Sorry kid. I can't be your dad."

"I'll go." Tom took his shirt off. "But you leave the girls alone."

Jimmy took a seat on the bank. "Good."

"Tom." I grabbed his arm. "What are you doing?"

He pulled me aside so we could talk alone. Jeanine walked along the bank. Suddenly, I wasn't afraid for my life anymore. I was scared Tom might lose his.

"Baby, I'll be all right." He took his shoes off next, then his pants hit the ground.

"You don't have to do this, you know." I swallowed the lump in my throat.

"Yes I do." He cradled my face. "For us. So one day we can have a family."

Even now, he'd remembered our conversation on the front porch. The day after a branch busted the window. When I'd been freaking out about that bloody note.

"We will be together." He kissed my hair. "I

promise."

I couldn't watch him swim with alligators. The thought alone sent a sharp chill up my spine. So when he stepped into the water, I turned my back and walked away.

I hated that necklace. And if it ever landed in my hands, I would destroy it myself.

As tears shook me to my core, I ran after Jeanine. She had followed the river upstream. And when I found her, she was lying down next to Ricky's body.

I ran my fingers through my hair and got down on my knees. Would this ever end?

I just wanted a regular life. To finish high school. Go to college. Get a job. Marry Tom. Have a family. But if fate kept twisting my arm, I would never get to do any of those things.

An alligator crept onto the bank and I screamed. "Jeanine!"

We each grabbed an arm and dragged Ricky away from the gator. But his body was heavy, and I didn't know if we would make it. I was out of breath, ready to give up.

"I can't do this!" Jeanine cried. "I can't watch that thing eat my brother!"

As it charged towards us, a gun went off. I ducked down and put my head between my legs. The bullets were so close, I swear one sailed right past my ear.

When I looked up, police swarmed. Jeanine was so shocked she passed out. But all I could think about was Tom. So I ran down the river bank and found DeMilo in handcuffs. They even had Hugh. But Jimmy was shaking hands with the police officers.

I looked in the river, and the green light was gone. But so was Tom.

All of the gators had disappeared. And I knew the reason why. Feeding time.

Heartbroken, I fell to my knees and cried out in agony. He was gone. The only man I'd ever loved. The only man who'd ever loved me. And man, had he known how to love.

Tom was rare. Because when he loved, he put his whole heart into it. And he had given me every piece of him. Except for a part I would never have. A part I wish I'd given when we had the chance. Now he was gone, and there was no turning back the clock.

Jimmy knelt down and pulled me into his arms. "They're going away for good."

"Are you really my father?" I looked up at him with weepy eyes.

He dried my tears. "Yeah, kid. I am."

I buried my face in his chest, so relieved to finally have a family. But had it come at the cost of losing Tom? I would never get over him. And this summer would haunt me forever.

"So are you the one who called the cops?" I asked.

Jimmy helped me to my feet. "No. That was all Tom."

"Well, I can't take all the credit for it."

I looked up as Tom came towards me. He was wearing his clothes, but his hair was dripping wet. When I ran into his arms, he picked me up and rubbed my back.

He was wincing by the time I finished squeezing him. Then I covered his face with kisses. But I'm sure he tasted a few tears, because my cheeks were stained with them.

"I thought you were dead," I sobbed.

"No." He ran his thumb along my jaw. "I would never leave you."

"You promise?" I admired his golden eyes. I never wanted them to go away.

"Yeah." He caressed my cheek. "I promise."

For the next two hours, the police took turns questioning us. Apparently, they had already gathered enough evidence to lock DeMilo and Hugh up for good. But with such a short life expectancy, I wasn't sure DeMilo would make it to the trial. Hugh was still young. By the time he was up for parole, he would be an old man.

They spent weeks searching for Nicki's body. But it never turned up.

That night, they put Ricky in a body bag and shipped him off to the examiner. Somehow, his death was worse this time around. You would have thought we'd all gotten used to it by now.

But when he'd come back, it felt like he'd never left. Even though I loathed Ricky for what he had done, there was a part of me that would always look for the good in him. Maybe because he was related to Tom. And I wished he could be a better man.

The next week, Emily was given a proper funeral. The one she deserved.

Eric gave a eulogy during the service. And I don't know how he made it through without crying. I balled my eyes out and put my head on Tom's chest. He wrapped one arm around Jeanine and the other around me, protecting the women in his life.

After the ceremony, I gave condolences to Emily's parents. We had always been close, and I was happy to have them back in Savannah. Eric would be attending Maple Creek High with us in the fall. And he wasn't even on speaking terms with Jeanine.

Once the church emptied, Eric caught us in the back. "That was beautiful," I said.

"Thanks." He shot a smile my way, and I reached out to give him a hug.

"I'm sorry, man." Tom slapped him on the back. "You did good today."

"Thanks." He was stalling, waiting for Jeanine to speak up.

"I'm sorry for your loss," she finally said. "Your sister was a good person."

"You never knew her," he replied. "But thank you anyway."

Jeanine cocked her head to the side. "Maybe I would have liked to know her."

"Well, why don't you talk to your brother about that?" he snapped.

She opened her mouth but didn't say anything.

"Your brother killed my sister," he said. "And I can't handle that."

Jeanine pierced his gaze with her bright blue eyes. "You killed my brother."

"Jeanine, you know why. Even the police said it was self-defense."

A tear ran down her cheek. "It was revenge. And I can't handle that."

Tom squeezed my side. "I think we'll just wait outside."

"You're not going anywhere," Jeanine said. But her eyes were on Eric.

"Well, I guess this means we can't be friends anymore."

"Yeah." Jeanine took a breath. "I guess not."

She walked out the door, and Eric watched her go.

"I'm so sorry." I touched his shoulder. "Don't give up on her."

"Yeah." Tom hugged me close. "She's stubborn like this one. But she'll come around."

"No." Eric shook his head. "Not about this."

When he left, the door slammed behind him. Tom looked down and put his arm around my shoulder. It had been a rough summer. I'd be happy when it was over.

"Come on." He kissed the corner of my mouth. "Let's go home."

Tom made pasta for dinner and then we curled up on the couch. Tonight would have been perfect for a movie. But he held me in his arms and we talked instead.

"What are we going to do about Eric and Jeanine?" I asked.

Tom shrugged, cradling my head in his lap.

"I mean, they're perfect for each other. We have to get them back together."

He laughed, tucking a lock of hair behind my ear.

"What?" I looked into his eyes. "Why are you laughing at me?"

"Because you're cute—wanting to get them back together."

"I know they like each other. Come on, they belong together!"

"If you say so." He bowed his head and planted a soft kiss on my lips.

I sat up and straddled his lap, resting my head on his chest. It felt so good to be in his arms again. For the next month, all I wanted was peace. Just a normal summer.

"I've been thinking..." Tom rubbed my lower back. "Why don't we plan a trip?"

"What kind of trip?" I asked. "Just the two of us? You and me?"

"Yeah." He kissed me, and I felt the grin on his lips.

"What about Eric and Jeanine?" I didn't want to abandon them now.

"With us gone, they'll be forced to reconcile their differences."

The doorbell rang, and I got off the couch. "Let me see who that is."

I opened the door to find Jimmy standing on the front porch. He smiled when he saw me, and I gave him a hug. It felt so good to have a true father. A real member of my family.

"Come on in." I stepped back in the doorway. "What are you doing here?"

"I wanted to pay you a visit. Oh, and I have something for you." He went on the porch and returned with a painting in his hands. It was Daniel's. The one I had wanted to buy.

"Jimmy." I put my hand over my heart. "You didn't have to do that."

"No, I wanted to." He set it against the wall in the foyer. "Daniel would've wanted you to have it. And there are more in the car. The portrait of your grandmother, too."

I shut the door. "There are a lot of questions I've been wanting to ask you."

"Okay." He nodded.

"Why don't you stay for a while?" I invited him into the living room where he shook Tom's hand. They were already well acquainted, since they had conspired to turn DeMilo into the police. Even I hadn't seen that one coming.

Jimmy had once asked me if I was going to marry Tom. And from the way they were interacting, I knew that my biological father had already approved.

We talked for hours. Jimmy was young when he met my biological mother, Josette. And he really did love her. But when she got pregnant, she disappeared out of his life.

By the time he knew I existed, Josette had already died. She had also chosen to give me up for adoption before the birth. A closed adoption with strict legal implications.

"I've wanted to contact you for so long," Jimmy said. "But I didn't know if you'd even want to meet me. And when I heard you were being raised by a doctor and a lawyer, I don't know. I guess I just got intimidated. I didn't want to mess up your life."

"You haven't messed up anything." I took his hand. "I wish you'd called sooner."

"Yeah." His eyes looked glassy. "Me too."

"So how come you're an artist, too?" I wondered. "Or is that just a coincidence?"

He grinned and lowered his lashes, flipping through the pages of his memory.

"Art is how your mother and I met. Daniel gave private lessons for a brief period. And I was one of his students. I came to his house, and he would teach me how to paint."

I was holding Tom's hand as Jimmy talked about her. My mother.

The woman I most wanted to meet, but never would.

"That was the first time I saw her. And when

she came down the stairs. Well, let me tell you, Addie." He cupped his chin in the palm of his hand. "She was really somethin'."

"I wish I could have met her." I teared up as Tom wrapped me in his arms.

"Yeah." Jimmy looked away with a smile. "I wish you could have, too."

"Have you had dinner?" I asked. "Tom is a great cook. He made pasta."

Jimmy hesitated.

"Please stay," I said. "I know you drove a long way to be here."

So he ate dinner and talked to us for hours at the kitchen table. Daniel had entrusted Jimmy with all of his secrets. That was how he knew about the necklace.

"Why did you take it?" I asked. "Hide the necklace in your office, I mean?"

"I thought it would be safe away from you. It was for your protection."

"But that put you at risk," I said. "Why would you put yourself in harm's way?"

He sat back in his chair. "I was just trying to protect you."

I thought about asking him why he never moved on after my mother. But watching him talk about her confirmed everything. He had given her his whole heart. And after her death, there was nothing left to give.

"Why don't you come back and see us some time?" I told Jimmy on his way out.

He shook Tom's hand. "Really?"

"Yes, really." I gave him a hug. "I would like that. A lot."

"Well, I'm glad." He stepped onto the porch and then turned around. "You know." He leaned against the railing. "I've actually been thinking about moving back to Savannah."

"That seems to be happening a lot around here lately," I said.

"Would you mind?" He looked at us. "Would it bother you if I was close?"

I went outside and kissed him on the cheek. "No," I whispered. "Not at all."

"Well, that's good, because I got a job offer from SCAD. Do you know what—"

"I know what SCAD is. The Savannah College of Art and Design," I smiled.

"Yeah."

"So, are you thinking about taking it?" I asked.

Jimmy looked at me with a straight face. "I already have."

I dove into his arms and hugged him close. He petted my hair as I cried. Despite the tears, I was so happy. Jimmy had finally given me all I ever wanted. A family.

"So I guess I'll be seeing a lot more of you then?" I leaned back.

"Yeah, I guess so." He patted my cheek. "I better get going."

"I love you, Dad." I hugged him one last time, breathing in his scent.

"I love you too, kid."

After he left, Tom and I watched a movie on the couch. As the opening credits began, I relaxed against him with a pleasant smile. Finally, so much of my life made sense.

Maybe I wasn't a mistake. Maybe I belonged to someone after all.

"I'm glad your dad is moving back," Tom said.

"So am I." I rubbed his arm. "Everything is perfect."

Tom winced, giving me a crooked grin. "I don't know about perfect."

"Close enough." I sighed when he kissed me.

Because it was.

## Chapter 24

In late July, Tom and I left on a romantic getaway to Myrtle Beach. I warned Eleanor beforehand this time. And she was gracious and kind, to my surprise.

"Of course you can go." She sat down with me at the kitchen table. "I'm sorry I've never been there for you, Addie."

When she started to tear up, I got all emotional. "Mom."

"Listen, I guess I'm just not the motherly type. But I just want what's best for you."

"Do you believe that's Tom?" I asked.

"Yes." She smiled and cupped my cheek. "Yes, I do. Just be careful and—"

"Mom. We've already had that talk."

"Right." She wiped her eyes. "I just want you to be safe."

"Mom, I am safe. With Tom."

"I know you are." She squeezed my hand. "He's lucky to have you."

"I'm lucky to have him."

Those were the high notes of our conversation. But I thought of them often on the road trip. Somehow, all of the danger had led Eleanor to trust us more. To treat us like adults instead of teenagers. Which was what I'd wanted all along.

It was late afternoon when we arrived. The water was so beautiful, it took my breath away. I rolled the window down and took a whiff of salty air.

It was heavenly. Peaceful. Just what I needed.

Tom rented a beach house in a secluded area. We had so much privacy, everyone probably thought we were honeymooners. When I stepped inside the place, I wasn't so sure that we weren't.

"Wow." There was a gorgeous view of the ocean from the living room. "Tom."

He had the biggest grin on his face as I walked to the window. After all the hell we'd been through, it felt like I was dreaming. Like it was too good to be true.

Tom came up behind me and put his head on my shoulder. Then he wrapped his arms around me and kissed my neck. "Do you like it?"

"Yes." I watched the waves as they came to shore. Crashing in the distance and then calming before they reached the sand. "I love it."

Tom put his hand to the glass. "That's all I ever wanted."

I looked up and caught him staring at me. "What?"

"For you to be happy."

"I am happy, Tom." I squeezed his hand. "I promise."

"Good." He kissed my cheek and gave me a hug. "Do you want to go on the beach?" He looked out at the water and pulled me into his side.

"Yeah." I tingled at the thought of showing him so much skin. Tom had never seen me in a bikini. Only because we'd never been in a situation where I needed to wear one.

"Then maybe we could go out to dinner?" He trailed his fingers down my neck. "I don't really feel like cooking tonight."

"Sure." I lost my breath. "That sounds fine."

Tom stayed in the bedroom, while I changed clothes in the adjoining bathroom. I took off my shirt in the mirror and thought about tonight. What if it finally happened? What if we finally had *sex*?

I slipped into my bikini bottoms and then tied the strings on the top. It was a new swim suit I'd bought for the occasion. And since I grabbed it off a Fourth of July sales rack, it looked pretty patriotic.

Red, white and blue. Stars and stripes. The top was mostly red with a bit of white trim. And the bottoms were navy blue.

I turned in the mirror and my heart jumped.

What would Tom do when he saw me in this? I knew what I wanted him to do.

Wanting to look good for him, I brushed my hair and reapplied some lip gloss. Except this time, I put on a deep red color. Like crimson.

I stalled in the bathroom for a few more minutes. Typically, I was very comfortable around Tom. But all of a sudden, I felt nervous.

When I came out, Tom was already on the beach. So I grabbed a couple towels and put on my sunglasses. Then I opened the sliding glass door and walked barefoot in the sand.

There were two beach chairs facing the ocean. I dropped the towels there and snuck up behind Tom. He was wearing black swim trunks, gazing out at the sea.

I circled my arms around his trim waist and pressed my cheek to his back. Tom turned around, and his hand slipped to the small of my back. In an instant, our torsos were flush.

And I loved it.

"Hi." He cupped my cheek in his hand and kissed me.

I pushed the weight of my body into him and molded my mouth to his. His lips were soft and sweet. And I couldn't get enough.

A breathy moan escaped me, as I ran my fingers through his hair. When he pulled away, I bit my tongue and whimpered. Tom grinned.

"What are you doing?" I asked.

He kicked up enough water to splash me. So I

waded into the sea and splashed him back. It took me a little while to figure out he was teasing me.

But I liked how good it felt. Especially when he picked me up in his arms. I dunked his head under the water, and he came up with me on his shoulders.

We were playing. And I couldn't remember the last time we had done something so normal. He captured me in his arms and coiled my legs around his waist.

"I've got you now," he spoke against my mouth.

"Yeah." I touched my nose to his. "You do."

\* \* \*

Tom had made reservations in advance. So when we drove to dinner, I knew it would be a nice place. I was wearing a summer dress with sandals. But Tom had on a tie.

"Are you sure this is okay?" I waved a hand over my outfit.

"I'm sure." He was wearing a button-down shirt and khakis. "It's fine."

We were seated immediately at the restaurant. Tom held my chair out for me and then took a seat. When the waiter came, Tom asked for more time to look over the menu.

There were so many options, I didn't know what to pick. But I was always in the mood for pasta. So I settled on fettuccine alfredo with chicken. And Tom ordered the same.

"Tom, this is beautiful." Our table was by a glass wall, so there was a crystal clear view of the ocean. The sun hadn't even set yet.

"Addie, I wanted to talk to you about something." He sounded so serious.

"Okay." I squeezed a lemon wedge into my water and stirred the glass with a straw. "What's up?"

"Well, I've been thinking." He folded his hands on the table. "We need to decide where we want to go to college."

I nodded, even though I hadn't expected this kind of talk from Tom. Eleanor had already given me the lecture. Senior year was approaching, and I needed to make a decision.

"Do you know where you want to go?" I asked.

"Well, that depends on you."

"I always planned on staying in state."

"All right. Well there's Georgia, Georgia Tech—"

"I think Georgia Tech was designed for people like you. No offense—it's just I'm no good at math and science."

He waved it off with a smile. "None taken."

"Wait...would that happen?"

"Would what happen?" Tom put a napkin in his lap as the waiter approached. He dropped our salads off and left.

"What if we don't get in to the same college?"

The corner of his mouth twitched. "Not to brag, but we both make pretty awesome grades.

I'm pretty sure it won't be a problem."

"No, I mean, what if we don't want to go to the same college?"

Tom smoldered. "I told you I would go wherever you go."

"But that's not fair." I shook my head. "We're not interested in the same things. What if I want to pursue my art? And what about your music?"

"Addie, you haven't painted in months. And when's the last time I picked up a guitar?" He set his fork down. "I have no problem majoring in something like chemistry."

I closed my eyes and sighed.

"Addie, I will find a major that works for me, I promise."

"But I don't want to make this decision for you. It's your choice."

"And I'm choosing to be with you. That's the most important thing to me."

"We're only seventeen," I reminded him. "You can't plan your whole life around me."

Tom threw his napkin on the table and slouched in his chair.

"I just want you to go to a college where you'll be happy," I said.

"Well, I'm not gonna be happy unless I'm with you." He got out of his chair and walked off. No one in the restaurant seemed to notice. He looked like he might be headed to the men's room. Not running from a difficult conversation with his girlfriend.

Five minutes passed, and I decided to go after him. There was no point in avoiding the inevitable. We'd have to fill out college applications soon. And if we couldn't talk about something as important as where we were headed next, what did that say about the relationship?

I found Tom on the pier outside. It extended from the restaurant out into the ocean. He was all alone, leaning on the wooden railing. I took a breath and moved towards him.

"I'm sorry." I waited for him to turn around. "I didn't know you were ready..."

He looked back over his shoulder. "Ready for what?"

I stood next to him and put my elbows on the railing. It really was beautiful out here. There was no storm tonight. The ocean was calm. At peace. Like I wanted us to be.

"Ready to talk about things like this," I said. "Big things."

Tom ran his hand over his face. "You really don't get it. Do you?"

I watched him, but he wouldn't meet my eyes. "Get what?"

"That I'm in love with you. And I'm never gonna stop wanting you."

I leaned in and put my hand on his chest. "I feel the same way."

"You sure don't act like it."

I pulled back and peered at the sun. "I'm sorry. Okay?"

He bowed his head and stared at the water down below.

"I'm sorry I haven't thought about college and what I want to major in, what I want to do with my life. I'm seventeen. I don't know. The only thing I do know is that I want to be with you. Forever." I put my hand over his. "And maybe you want that, too?"

"Yes." He drew my body into his. "I've always wanted that."

"I don't know about all that other stuff." I wrapped my arms around his back. "But if there's one thing I'm serious about—it's you."

He leaned his forehead against mine. "I'm pretty serious about you, too."

When I touched his face, Tom sealed his lips over mine. It was the perfect kiss. The kind you see at the end of a movie. And it makes you jealous, because you want that for yourself.

"I'm sorry." I looked into his eyes. "I may not know everything, but I really do love you." Our cheeks brushed as I gave him a hug. "I've always loved you."

He pulled back and caressed my face. "I've always loved you, too."

Reconciled, we walked back to the restaurant hand in hand. Then we ate dinner and watched the sun set. By the time we reached the beach house, I was mostly sleepy from consuming complex carbohydrates. No matter how creamy and delicious they were.

But I was mostly something else, too.

"Don't worry about all that college stuff, baby." Tom shut the door. "Now probably wasn't the best time to bring it up. I have no doubt in my mind we'll figure it out."

"Me too," I smiled, following him into the bedroom.

I took my sandals off and sat down on the bed. It had been a long day, but I was happy to be here with Tom. All summer, it felt like we'd never been able to enjoy each other.

As Tom removed his tie, I got to thinking. "You know, I'm really glad it's all over."

"What?" Tom bent over to untie the laces on his shoes.

"Everything. DeMilo. Ricky. That *stupid* necklace." I got up. "I can't tell you how happy I am that it's finally done. I don't have to think about it anymore. It's over."

Tom stepped out of his shoes and leaned on the dresser.

"And you." I ran my hands down his shirt. "I'm so proud of you."

He put his hand on my waist and smiled when I kissed him. "Why?"

"Because you're so brave," I whispered in his ear.

"I don't know about that," he said. "But I did everything I could to protect you."

"I know you did." I pulled him away from the dresser. "And I want to reward you."

I unzipped my dress and it fell to the floor. His eyes traveled down my body. And when they lingered in certain places, I felt flushed. But I kicked my dress to the side anyway.

"Addie," he said hoarsely. Five seconds and he was already out of breath.

That had to be a good sign.

"I want you." I ran my hand down his arm. "I don't want to wait anymore."

He had no words. So I kissed him and curled my arms around his neck. For some reason, there was a little resistance on his end. And I couldn't figure out why.

"Touch me." I kissed the pulse point in his neck. "I want you to touch me."

And that was his undoing. He cradled my face in his hands, tender and gentle at first. But that pace had proved unsuccessful in the past. So I pushed Tom on to the bed and climbed on top of him.

"Take your clothes off," I whispered. "Please."

He unbuttoned his shirt, and I helped him push down the sleeves. Then he sat up against the headboard and weaved his fingers through my hair. I sat down in his lap and trailed kisses down his chest. He tensed up and pressed his fingertips into my back.

"Do you know why this is going to be perfect?" I asked.

"Why?" Tom was gasping for air. Especially when I kissed him again.

"Because you're honest." I kissed his abs. "And I know you would never lie to me."

Tom leaned his head back and stared off into space. He wasn't into this.

"Are you okay?" I kissed his face and neck.

"Yeah." He couldn't look me in the eye. "Sorry. I'm fine."

But he didn't seem fine. "Then why aren't we naked yet?"

Tom pushed off me and got out of bed. "Addie."

I wrapped the sheet around me, feeling rejected again.

He scratched his head and looked out the window.

"I thought you wanted me," I murmured. "I thought you wanted this."

"Baby, I do." He spun around and held my hand. "Trust me, I do."

"Then what's wrong?" I felt like crying. "Why won't you love me?"

He cupped my cheek in his hand. And I kissed the inside of that hand.

"There is something I have to tell you." He stood up. "Get dressed." He put his shirt back on and then pushed the sliding glass door open. "Meet me on the beach."

Of all the times we'd been interrupted... And now he was the one who wanted to stop. Because apparently there was something else more important. I was so frustrated I wanted to scream.

But we still had what was left of the weekend. So I kept it inside for now.

I slipped into my dress and pulled the sliding glass door shut behind me. Tom was waiting on the shoreline. And as my feet sank into the cool sand, I let out a sigh.

"Hey." I reached him and put my hands on my waist. "What's going on?"

Tom took a deep breath and shut his eyes. Then he put his hands in his pockets. I couldn't understand what was going on. Until he dropped something cold in my hand.

"I didn't give the necklace to the police," he said.

"But I thought you said—"

"I told them it got lost in the river."

I looked at the necklace in my hand. "Why would you lie?"

"Because I don't trust them." He watched me. "Do what your dad said, Addie."

"What?" I looked up at Tom, tearing myself away from the enchanting emerald.

"Throw it in the ocean." He lowered his voice. "So no one will ever find it."

I furrowed my brow as tears burned the back of my eyes. "I don't understand."

"You want to get rid of it?" he asked. "You want this thing out of our lives?"

I nodded.

"Then throw it in." He nodded towards the sea. "You'll never have to see it again."

Somehow, I felt guilty for wanting to toss it. There was no telling how much the necklace was worth. But it wasn't about the money. It was a gift, an heirloom.

How could I get rid of my grandmother's necklace?

"But Antoinette—I mean, my grandmother. It's all I have of her."

"It won't bring her back," he said. "And even she would want you to be safe."

I cradled the emerald in my hand—like it was my own heart. Then I looked up and saw my future in his eyes. Suddenly, it all became very clear. What I had to do.

"We won't ever talk about this again," I said. "It'll be like it never happened."

"Yeah." Tom nodded, guiding me into the water. "Like it never happened."

I looked at the necklace and then saw lightning on the horizon.

"A storm is coming," Tom said. "A pretty bad one."

I watched the tide coming in. Then I took a deep breath and threw the necklace into the ocean. It flickered beneath the moonlight, gracefully plopping into the rapids.

"You did the right thing." Tom rubbed my back.

"Did I?"

"Yeah." He led me off the sand. "It's over now."

I wanted to cry, because it felt like I was losing Daniel all over again.

"Come on." Tom tugged at my hand. "Let's go back."

I walked with him to the beach house. But once Tom went inside, I looked back. And I thought I saw something in the distance. It was a light. Luminescent. Bright and green.

Maybe it was the necklace. Maybe it wasn't. I would never see the emerald again.

But for the first time, I was okay with that. I could accept it.

Because some doors are better left unopened.

# Epilogue

**M**aple Creek High in the fall. Not my favorite part of the year. But we had to go back at some point. Summer couldn't last forever. And I knew that now more than ever.

This semester, Eric Kent was the new kid in town. But his homecoming wasn't well received. Every time he walked down the hall, there wasn't a student who didn't stop and stare. He was ostracized, kept at a distance, feared by the general public.

*I heard he killed someone.*

*You murdered Travis.*

*He scares me.*

Eric heard it every day of the week. Since Tom and I associated with him, the censure touched us as well. People called us freaks. Even Jeanine was exposed to the treatment.

Regardless, we kept on plowing through our

daily lives. Jeanine and Eric had yet to reconcile. So Tom and I were left to hang out with one of them or the other.

We weren't picking sides. So if Jeanine walked up, Eric would leave. And vice versa.

The worst part? I think they really cared about each other.

But how do you move past something like that? It wasn't like they'd had a silly argument. Ricky murdered Emily. And then Eric killed Ricky.

It was a twisted thing—losing a sibling to each other. But I held on to the hope of their reunion. Eric showed no interest in dating any of the girls at Maple Creek High. I doubt any of them would go out with him anyway. They were too afraid of him.

Some days, I dropped Jeanine off after school. And then Tom would hang out with Eric. I wasn't sure what they talked about. Probably us—we were talking about them.

"I can't get it out of my head." Jeanine walked into Ricky's room.

"It was self-defense. Eric is a good person. He would never—"

"Maybe so." She sat down on the bed. "But you can't tell me he didn't like it."

"Jeanine." I knelt down in front of her. "Eric is not a murderer."

"Then why is my brother dead?" she asked.

"We're just gonna have to work through this. Okay? I'm so sorry."

When she cried, I held her close. It was strange being in Ricky's room. So we went downstairs for some milk and cookies. She had been spending more time with her grandmother. And that was where the goodies came from. For that, I was glad.

"Addie, I want to tell you something." Jeanine hopped up on the counter. "After Ricky died, I went through his things. And I found all these letters in his room."

I leaned against the stove and crossed my arms over my chest.

"They were from Paris. Did you know he spoke fluent French?"

"Ricky?" I was shocked. "No. I had no idea."

"Well, he found a buyer for the necklace. He was planning on selling it."

"What?" I shook my head. "But DeMilo. He was sick. He—"

"I know, I know." She got something out of her pocket. "I found that the night he died." It was a crumpled message. "It was in his pocket."

Curious, I unraveled the paper "I can't read this. It's in French."

Jeanine pulled out her laptop and typed Google into the browser. Then she looked at the message and entered it into a translator. My heart was racing. What did it mean?

*J'ai trouvé le collier.*

I found the necklace.

## Tell Me Your Favorite Part!

If you enjoyed Honey Gold, I invite you to head over to Amazon and let me know your favorite part. Reviews are so important to an author's career, because they help new readers like you discover the book. Even if you didn't enjoy Honey Gold, I'd still love it if you could take three minutes to let me know what you think of the book.

### Leaving a review is super easy:

1) Go to Honey Gold Book Page on Amazon

2) Scroll Down and click "Write a Customer Review"

3) Sign in to Amazon if prompted

4) Select a star rating

5) Write a few short words (or long words, I won't judge)

6) Click the 'submit' button

I thank you in advance!

## Acknowledgements

I would like to start by thanking the reader. Without you, none of this would be possible. Thank you for reading my books and spreading the word. You are the reason why writing love stories is so special to me—because you are ready and waiting to read them. And I can never thank you enough for that.

To my parents, family and close friends. Thanks for sticking by my side. Your love and support has truly meant the world to me. Can't wait to see you all soon.

To the amazing authors—Micalea Smeltzer, Molly E. Lee, Aubrey Parr, Amanda Leigh, Lauren L. Garcia. We're always there to support and encourage each other. And I will always adore the indie author community for that.

Special thanks to Colleen Noyes and Kylie Frankel. Thank you so much for getting my books into the hands of readers. I would also like to thank Susan Meachen, Teri Hicks, Margie Fite, Rose Marie Newport, Aurora Hale and Jessica Hernandez.

Much love to my Lucky Stars. You are my super fans, and I can't thank you enough for coming along on this crazy ride with me. I love connecting with you each and every day. And I'm looking forward to making so many awesome memories in the years to come!

## About the Author

Lindsay Marie Miller was born and raised in Tallahassee, Florida, where she graduated from high school as Valedictorian. At sixteen, she started writing her first novel, *Emerald Green*, after being inspired by Stephenie Meyer's International Bestselling *Twilight Saga*. During her time in college, Lindsay wrote 5 more novels and over 100 songs. After graduating Summa Cum Laude from Florida State University, she put her B.A. in English Literature to good use and published her debut novel, *Emerald Green*. An author of over 10 Romance Titles, Lindsay currently resides in her hometown of Tallahassee where she is always working on her next novel.

### To learn more, please visit:

www.lindsaymariemillerauthor.com

### Sign up for Lindsay's newsletter:

lindsaymariemillerauthor.com/claim-your-free-book/

### Join Lindsay on Facebook at:

facebook.com/LindsayMarieMillerAuthor

### Follow Lindsay on Twitter at:

twitter.com/Lindsay_MMiller

# LOOK FOR THE NEXT BOOK

## AVAILABLE

## JANUARY 2018